UNFORGETTABLE MAN

TIYE LOVE

Garden Avenue Press

QUOTE

*Love
Is a ripe plum
Growing on a purple tree.
Taste it once
And the spell of its enchantment
Will never let you be.*

- Langston Hughes

Unforgettable Man by Tiye Love

Copyright © 2020, Tiye Love

Garden Avenue Press

Atlanta, Georgia

ISBN: 978-1-946302-38-0 (Ebook edition)

ISBN: 978-1-946302-39-7 (Paperback edition)

This book is a work of fiction. All names, characters, locations, and incidents are products of the author's imagination, or have been used fictitiously. Any resemblance to actual persons living or dead, locales, or events is entirely coincidental. No part of this e-book may be reproduced or shared by any electronic or mechanical means, including but not limited to printing, file sharing, and e-mail, without prior written permission from Tiye Love.

I
ROYALTY

"This evening is a brand new start for Deaux's Auto. Our most troubled youth will have an opportunity for a second or even third chance for a bright future by learning hands-on auto mechanic and entrepreneur skills. My future wife and I will continue the legacy of her father, Wayne Thibodeaux, and help our youth get a fresh new start. With your help, we can really effect the change we need to make the great city of New Orleans a pioneer in juvenile reform. We thank you again for such an amazing turnout."

The supportive audience of family, friends, policymakers, social workers, and locals in the neighborhood clapped enthusiastically as Tre LaSalle, the mayor of New Orleans, and my best friend's fiancé, finished speaking. We were outside her father's old repair shop that had been revamped with Tre's money to be used as a center for wayward youth. He had totally transformed the shop that had been abandoned years ago into a fully functioning four-bay modern repair shop that would rival any major competitor.

People gathered around to congratulate and take pictures with the handsome young mayor. Standing near the street on the fringe of the event, I observed Raini beaming proudly at his side.

My heart swelled every time I saw them together. They were still in the throes of new love, the type of love I've always wanted where neither wanted to be apart from each other. I'd remained single because I had yet to find that special man who made me believe that fairytales do come true and that he would always be my prince.

"Why are you over here all alone?" Anthony, my current lover, walked up to me with a glass of champagne.

"I needed a moment. Raini's father had been a dad to me, too. This shop brings back so many memories of a happier time. Life really was simpler back then." I used a Kleenex tissue to wipe my eyes, careful not to smudge my makeup. I don't know why I didn't use waterproof mascara when I knew I would be a blubbering bubbling mess.

He patted my back, attempting to soothe me. "Do you want me to get you some wine or food?"

"Sure. It doesn't matter what you bring me," I answered, more for him to leave me alone than any desire to eat or drink.

He strode inside the lobby of the garage that had been transformed into a lively reception area with a band. I'd met Anthony at the gallery the night of Raini's art show. I only entertained him initially to avoid Devin Toussaint, a man I briefly dated years ago, who'd kept trying to get me alone that night. Once he saw me talking to Anthony, he left the event. I hadn't seen him again, though he sent me flowers at work and periodically asked to see me. I held on to each of his cards though I never called him, not to even thank him for the flowers.

Anthony kept me engaged after Devin left the gallery, and I decided to give him a real chance. We'd been dating non-exclusively for three months, and he looked good on paper with his nice home in the suburbs of New Orleans, his Beamer, and a degree in geology which he used to work on ships deep in the gulf, analyzing the richness of oil.

In person, he was boyishly attractive, with walnut brown skin, a slim build, and light brown eyes hidden behind wire-rimmed glasses. We had a good time when we were together, good conversation, good in bed...everything about him was good. Yet, I found myself yearning for something more. My mother said I was too picky, that no man was perfect. Easy for her to say because she'd been lucky to find her perfect man when she was twenty.

My father had been on leave from the Navy when he stopped in the soul food café where she worked as a waitress. And thirty-six years, two children and one grandson later, they were living in Okinawa still blissfully in love. My older brother followed in my father's footsteps and had been in the Navy for years, currently stationed in San Diego, divorced, no children, and seemingly happy.

Overall, I've enjoyed my life. Juggling motherhood and school had been tough, but now that Ryder was older, independent, more self-sufficient at ten years old, I could breathe more. I had had relationships, even a couple of serious ones, but at thirty-four I still hoped for that special man. Thought I met him once.

I shook my head. I didn't need to think about Devin. He was no good for me or for any self-respecting woman. Even if he was, unknowingly, the father of my son.

Misinterpreting my head shake, Anthony, who'd returned with a glass of red wine and crab puffs, asked, "Did you want white?"

"It doesn't..."

Suddenly, I felt someone's stare and turned in that direction. I blinked back unexpected tears at the only man who made me smile just at the sight of him. Down the street, Devin Toussaint, sharply dressed in a gray suit, leaned on his midnight blue Maserati.

I looked back at Anthony. "Yeah. Could you get me white, and I don't like the puffs? You know what, just go back inside and I'll meet you."

Anthony frowned but turned and headed back into the

makeshift reception area. I instantly searched for my son, Ryder, grateful he had been obsessed with the model cars in the garage and had been inside the shop for most of the event. I then hurried to Raini, who stood near Tre as he now spoke with reporters.

I asked in her ear, "Hey...why is Devin here?"

"Where is he?" Raini worriedly glanced at her fiancé and then back at me.

"He's down the street, beside his car. You can't see him from here. You don't think he's here to start any trouble?"

Raini responded, "Doubtful. He told me that he knew my father. Maybe he's here to pay respects."

"You're sure he isn't still trying to get at you? He can be persistent."

She smiled. "Ask him yourself. Stop playing hard to get when we both know you're still crazy about him."

I didn't bother to deny. "He's dangerous."

Raini whispered, "Dangerous? Why would he be dangerous?"

"It's not important. I'm going to see why he's here. Can you keep an eye on Ryder? I don't want Devin to know that I have a son."

Raini pulled me farther away from the dwindling crowd and scrutinized my face. "I know we haven't had time to really talk since I moved in with Tre, and we can't get into this right now. But isn't it time you're honest with Devin?"

The contents of my stomach rumbled around, though I calmly asked, "Why? Ryder and I are just fine."

Tre called for Raini. She held one finger up to him and looked at me. "Royalty, no matter what, I love you. I see the resemblance between Ryder and Devin, and sooner or later so will other people. Your secret is safe with me...for now."

I bit my lip, real fear hitting me. I hadn't shared with anyone that Devin was the father of my son, not even with my best friend, but she'd figured it out. What if he did see me with Ryder —a son I had never told him about? Common sense alone would make him ask who's the father, and Devin had an abundance of both book and common.

I inhaled deeply and glanced around me to make sure no one watched me as I headed down the street. He was, after all, Tre's enemy.

The closer I moved toward him, I could see that he'd been crying. Unblinking with teary eyes, Devin shifted his stance and smiled in greeting. He seemed vulnerable, and that was an emotion I thought he was incapable of feeling.

I greeted him. "Hey. How long you been here?"

"Not long. No worries, Royalty, I'm about to leave. Tell Raini I didn't come to start trouble."

I rubbed my arms to fight off the thrilling chill that coursed through my body at the rumble of his deep voice, before hugging myself in relief. He didn't see me with Ryder. "Then why are you here?"

"I hadn't been to his shop in years. Used to come here almost every day at one point," Devin said quietly, before averting his gaze past my shoulders. "I wanted to be here for Deaux."

I shifted from foot to foot, standing across from him, keeping my distance, knowing that to be any closer would be certain death for me. "How did you know him?"

Devin unbuttoned his suit jacket as he responded. "He helped me when I needed it the most." He then pulled his jacket off, his muscular frame visible through his tapered white button-up shirt that made a stark contrast against his dark chocolate skin, and moved closer to me, placing it around my sweater-covered shoulders. "Better?"

I resisted closing my eyes at the warmth and smell of his expensive cologne emanating from the material around me. "You're going to be cold now." The temperature had been steadily dropping as day made way to evening, and it had been a cold night even for a January in New Orleans.

Devin shrugged and returned to his position against his car. "As long as you're warm." He inhaled deeply and looked toward

5

the event. "It looks like a nice crowd. Deaux meant a lot to this community, even when he ran the streets. That man stayed on my ass and sometimes I miss him like he just died."

His honest admission surprised me. "Yeah, I miss him so much, too." I fought the tears that had been falling most of the day. "With my own father gone so much in the military, Deux was my father, too. God knows that he gave me and Raini hell about being the best students and leaving those raggedy boys alone who only wanted one thing. I had to hear his mouth whenever me and Raini wanted to go somewhere. Crazy how we knew the same man, who meant a lot to both of us, but didn't know it." I sniffed.

Devin's jaw tightened as he studied me. "Not surprised. You and I didn't do a lot of talking."

My stomach twisted painfully at the reminder of the fiery chemistry between us. Hugging myself tighter, I returned my focus on the event and watched some of the participants head back to their cars. "Maybe you should leave now. If Tre sees you, he'll be pissed."

He pushed off his car and I took a step back. "I don't give a fuck about Tre. As far as I'm concerned, the only good thing he's done since he's been in office is clear Deaux's name and re-dedicate his shop. Deaux and that place over there saved my life. I'll be damned before I let anyone keep me from paying my respects. I'm only keeping my distance for Raini's sake."

Surprised at the sudden attack of jealousy I experienced as he said my best friend's name with such admiration, I said, "You know she really loves Tre."

He met my direct gaze. "The whole city knows."

I folded my arms and warned, "She only has eyes for him."

Devin responded smoothly, "And I only have eyes for you."

The seriousness in his expression caught the sarcastic retort before the words left my mouth. We stared at each other for a long, silent moment. His gaze drifted to my lips, and when he slowly lowered his head, I yearned for his kiss. I closed my eyes, expecting the fullness of his lips on mine, but instead felt the soft caress of his mouth on my cheek. I opened my eyes, expecting to see his devilish smirk. All that I witnessed was longing.

He spoke gruffly, "I better go. Wouldn't want to cause confusion between you and your man."

"Man?" I backed up to the curb as he opened his door and he lowered himself into his car.

"I just saw you with that same lucky man at the gallery," Devin responded before his engine sprang to life.

"Lucky?"

"You're his." He then closed the door firmly, and I watched until he turned the corner, uncaring that he was probably doing the same in his rearview mirror. Belatedly, I realized I still had his jacket. I wrapped myself in his essence, walking slowly back, pretending it was his strong arms.

2

DEVIN

"Oh...shit...baby, you feel so fucking good," Reecie cooed as I stroked her deep and hard from the back.

I had her face down, ass up on my desk, as I pumped fiercely, trying to reach an elusive climax because I couldn't get a beautiful, stubborn woman out of my damn head.

Royalty haunted my dreams. I needed to see her again, and since she refused to give me her personal number, I had called her a few times at her job, to no avail. Besides the flowers I'd been sending since I first saw her months ago, I spent three hundred dollars on a special bouquet I had sent to her office, the day after I saw her again at Deaux's. Thinking of how hot sex used to be with her spiked my libido, and in a few seconds, I came right before Reecie screamed her satisfaction.

I pulled out of her, lifted my pants, and went into the bathroom attached to my office to dispose of my condom and clean myself. When I walked back into my office, Reecie had pushed down her dress and reapplied her lipstick.

She smiled and grabbed me to her, running her hand over my back and ass before wrapping her arms around my waist. "It's still early. You want to catch dinner?"

I sighed internally, regretful that I let my dick rule my brain once again. "No."

"Just 'no,' you can't even suggest another time we can hang out?"

I looked down at her and calmly repeated, "No. I already have plans."

She removed her hands, and her face contorted into disgust. I knew Reecie well enough to recognize that she was gearing up for an argument that I had no desire to engage in. "Reecie...you need to move on. We will never be more than this."

"You've been divorced. Why can't you get over her? You're not even trying. All you do is fuck around and won't give any woman a chance."

I stepped back to lean against my desk and met the angry eyes of the golden skinned, beautiful Reecie, used to having any man she wanted. Except me. "I've been over my ex-wife. We married for the wrong reasons anyway."

Reecie whined, "Then why can't we be more?"

Because you'll never be Royalty, I wanted to shout, but instead said to her, "I don't want more."

"I don't know why I keep allowing you to use me. The minute you come, you forget my fucking name."

I rubbed my hand over my beard. "You texted me under the false pretense that you had a case you wanted to discuss. You get here and the next thing I know, my dick is in your mouth. I didn't lie or mislead you. If you didn't want just sex with me, don't come to my office offering me nothing but your body. I used to be a selfish asshole, promising women things I had no intention of delivering, but I'm not that guy anymore. I've always been honest with you. It's just sex between us. If you want a relationship, then I'm not that man."

"You're still a selfish bastard." Her face crumpled. "You keep doing this to me. Making me think that we have something. Why did you fuck me again, huh?"

Aggravated, I said, "Honestly, I don't know why since we keep having this conversation."

I felt the piercing sting of her palm on my cheek. My hands balled into fists at the unexpected pain, and I inhaled deeply, forcing my hands to relax. "It's time for you to go. We're not going to do this anymore. I won't call you and for damn sure lose my number." I threw her jacket at her. "Get the hell out of my office."

"I fucking hate you." She angrily donned her jacket and her heels.

I stood by my now opened door, arms folded across my chest, uncaring that Reecie had begun to cry. "You're not the first woman to tell me that."

"One day, you're going to meet someone who's going to break your fucking heart."

Thinking of Royalty, I retorted, "I already did. Your point?"

Reecie screamed in frustration. I picked up her purse and handed the large expensive designer bag to her. She snatched the straps from me and marched out of the office and, hopefully, my life.

"Damn, Dev, what happened to your face?" my cousin Nicholas asked once I opened the front door to my office an hour later.

I gestured for him to sit on the sofa in the comfortable living/reception area. I purchased a five-bedroom home a few years ago and converted it into an office building in the mid-city area of New Orleans. I'd spent so much time in my office, I wanted my workspace to be my home away from home.

I plopped down next to him on the mustard sofa. "Reecie."

He frowned. "You still fucking her?"

"Not anymore." Pointing to my face, I responded, "Hence the bruise."

"Good thing it's Thursday. By Saturday, no one will notice." I waved my hand. "I've had worse scars."

He shook his head ruefully. "You and these women."

"Like you not out here in these streets knocking them out left and right."

Nicholas, with his light brown skin and eyes, muscular build, and winning smile, had been a chick magnet since middle school. "Cuz, I don't have the problems you have with women. It's like one time with you and they lose their minds."

"Most days I can't tell if it's a gift or a curse." I dropped my head back against the sofa. "I'm tired of women thinking I'm playing games when I'm not. Damn if I do or don't."

"What happened?"

"Reecie texted me saying she wanted to discuss some business with me and asked could she stop by my office. One thing led to another. When she wanted to hang out later, I told her I had plans. She accused me of leading her on then slapped the piss out of me. I had to kick her out my office before I ended up with a case. Shit, I've been hit when I've lied *and* when I'm telling the truth. I'm done with women."

Nicholas burst out laughing.

"I'm serious. I need a break from the drama."

"Dev, you're the biggest hoe I know. You're done until your dick gets hard again, which will be tomorrow when the next sexy-ass woman passes your way."

I chuckled at his accurate assessment of the old me. The new me hadn't had sex in months, trying to wait for a certain mocha vixen, which is probably why I even bothered with Reecie in the first place. Lack of sex had screwed up my decision-making ability. "Not anymore. I'm too old for this shit, dealing with these crazy-ass women."

"Or maybe we're the ones driving them crazy."

I turned my head to look at my cousin, and we dapped each other before saying together loudly, "Naw."

"You know we're in complete denial, right?" Nicholas commented.

Sighing loudly, I acknowledged, "Okay...okay. I'm not proud of my past treatment of women. I've learned my lesson, and I am done with all of them except one."

He smiled knowingly. "Except one? Just one?"

Nodding, I explained. "Real talk. I used to kick it with this bad-ass woman years ago until she cut off communication. I bumped into her at the French Market a few months ago, and she just might be the next Mrs. Toussaint."

"'Mrs. Toussaint'? You're feeling her like that? Seriously?"

"Real talk. Ever since I ran into her again, I can't get her out of my mind. She's a brilliant attorney who's grown sexier and even more beautiful. It's driving me crazy because she won't give me the time of day. I've been sending her flowers for months now. I saw her at that dedication for Deaux's Auto last week, and I gave her my favorite suit coat to wear because it was cold. She still has it, and I don't care. And you know how I am about my clothes."

My cousin whistled. "You really do like her."

"Between you and me, think I may already love her. I was falling for her even back then when she tossed me to the curb."

His wide forehead furrowed. "When was this? I don't remember any woman having you wide open, not even your ex-wife."

"I met her in D.C while she was there for school, though she's from New Orleans."

"Dev, I asked when did this happen? I didn't ask where you met her. I'm trying to figure out why you didn't get with this woman back then?"

At my silence, he peered into my face. "You were married, weren't you?"

I slunk down on the sofa. "Yeah."

"Then that's why she ghosted you."

"She didn't know I was married. We never discussed personal

lives. I flew up to see her a couple weekends a month the summer I met her."

"Come on, dude. Women always have a way of finding out about these things." He tapped his knee. "So, she married now?'

"No, but she has a man. Don't know too much more than that. She's not on social media."

"If she has a man then leave her alone. He might be a good dude.

"And I'm not?"

He stared at me, unblinking.

I protested, "I can be."

"Cuz, you're good with people, always giving back to the community, you're good at your career and one of the toughest litigators in the country, but being monogamous is not a part of your vocabulary. Not judging you, it's not a part of mine either."

My cousin, at thirty-six, had never had the desire to be married or have children. He enjoyed his freedom too much to settle down. Besides, like myself, he didn't have a healthy representation of marriage growing up. His parents had been teenagers forced to marry because of their families and divorced as soon as they could so they both could run the streets doing whatever the hell they wanted, leaving my cousin to his own devices. My father worried about his only nephew, finally gained custody when Nicholas was thirteen, and brought him to live with us when I had just turned fifteen.

We had become more like brothers than cousins ever since. He majored in public policy and engineering, while I studied law. Nicholas had been the Chief Technology Officer for the city of New Orleans while my father was mayor. Now he ran a political consulting firm.

"Being faithful to one woman ain't so bad. I did it once me and Nia got back together after we separated."

"That only lasted a couple of years before you cheated with your side piece again, and your wife left you again."

"I only fucked around because I knew Nia started back up

with Justin." Surprisingly, it didn't hurt anymore to talk about my ex-wife and her new husband. While we were separated, she'd fallen in love and gotten pregnant by Justin Ray, a popular singer. We reconciled for two years before he came back into our lives and she ultimately decided to leave me for him. "I enjoyed the last two years of our marriage, wished I'd been a better husband."

"You probably would have cheated on her again eventually because you didn't really love Nia the way that a husband should love a wife."

"She still deserved my fidelity whether we were right for each other or not. Thinking I fucked up my marriage so bad, I haven't been able to find real love. Karma can be the biggest bitch."

"What is wrong with you? All pessimistic and shit. This is not my cuz, talking like this."

"It is. You can't do people wrong and expect good things." I straightened up against the sofa. "I want a wife again."

"If that's all, you can get a wife. The way these women be after you, you could be married tomorrow."

"I know that. But I want a woman who loves me for me. I married Nia because she came from the same type of family and didn't care about my name or my possessions. At one point, she loved me, and I had a glimpse of what a good marriage could be, and I want that again. *This* woman would love me for me, and I would love the hell out of her. Maybe she would want to even have my baby." The idea of Royalty wearing my name and carrying my seed made me smile.

"You still miss Nya?"

My smiled faded, thinking about the child I reared until she was two. Then Justin, her biological father, returned and wanted custody and my wife. "Yeah, today Nia sent me some pics of her. She's getting so big. It fucked with me, and I wanted to escape, which is probably why I let Reecie suck me off in the first place and she somehow flipped it like I lied to her."

"Next time get drunk or bake if you want to escape. Pussy gets you in trouble...unless you're Derrick Toussaint."

"I wish I could argue." My father was and continues to be a notorious player with seemingly no consequences. My mother is his second wife—after his first wife couldn't take his infidelity—and has tolerated his behavior for years. She's partially why I thought it was acceptable for me to cheat on Nia. She would yell, curse him, snatch me out of bed in the middle of the night swearing she was done with him, but he would buy her a gift or promise he would do better, and she would forgive him.

My parents been together forty long years of marital dysfunction. I'm never impressed when I hear couples proudly discuss how many years they've been together unless they're happy. My former father-in-law and his wife have a strong marriage, and so do Tre's parents. I wanted what they had, something true, something real, something lasting.

Nicholas interrupted my thoughts. "It's not my place, but maybe you should stop torturing yourself and let Nya go. She and Nia are living in Atlanta now and have moved on, so it's time you do, too."

My voice rose as I explained, "I was her daddy for two years, the first one to hold her when she came into this world, missed out on sleep when she was sick, changed her dirty diapers, taught her how to use a sippy cup. She held *my* hand trying to take her first steps. She called me 'dada' and preferred me before she even called Nia 'mama.' It doesn't matter if she doesn't remember me, I'll always remember her and want the best for her."

He held his palm out placatingly. "Chill, cuz. I know how much she meant to you. We all miss Nya, too. She was part of our family, and it devastated us all when you admitted she wasn't yours. Just noticing that you get like this anytime you hear from Nia, wishing for a different life when the one you have is a good one."

"I want a better one with my own family."

"I hear you." Nicholas pressed his fist against mine. "Do you, Devin, do you. So, who is this woman who got you waxing poetic and wanting to put a ring on it?"

My spirits lifted simply at the thought of her. "She's Raini Blue's best friend, and her name is Royalty."

"Nice name." He paused a beat. "Wait...Tre's Raini?"

"How many Raini Blues do you know? We actually ran into each other again because of Raini."

He whistled. "That maybe why she ain't trying to holla at you. I'm sure Tre has some *nice* things to say about you."

Confidently I said, "Yeah, but Raini likes me for Royalty because I knew Deaux, and to her that means I'm worth a shot. I'm banking that Royalty will listen to her best friend before Tre."

"Good luck with that. Blood between you and Tre is really bad." Nicholas jumped up. "Come on, enough talk about this love nonsense. We should be on our third beers. If we leave now, we can make in time for the second quarter of the Knicks game."

"It's a nice night, let's just walk down to Vincent's Bar and catch the game there." I joined my cousin, and we headed out the door.

3
ROYALTY

While on hold, waiting to speak with Ryder's principal, I picked up a purple rose from the bouquet Devin sent me and smelled the sweet fragrance, wondering at what point I'd gather the strength to tell him about Ryder. Thinking that maybe I had misjudged him all those years ago and that I'd been more than sex to him. More importantly, maybe had I told him the truth back then, he would have been there for me and our son.

"Ms. James?"

"Yes." I placed the flower on my organizer.

"We need to have a conference about Ryder's behavior. I don't know how much longer we can tolerate his antics."

I groaned, pushing my chair back from my desk, thinking I didn't need this shit today. I had a deadline that I needed to meet yesterday. "What did Ryder do this time?"

The calm yet authoritative voice answered, "He's being disrespectful to his teacher."

"Let me guess, Mrs. Nelson?"

"Yes. We have zero tolerance for insolent behavior."

"My son is a lot of things, but insolent he isn't. I do need to meet with Mrs. Nelson to understand her definition of 'disrespectful' anyway. Ryder has made complaints about her, as well."

"Please do so. If his behavior continues—"

I interrupted impatiently, "Dr. Bennett, I am fully aware of the rules. One of the partners in my firm sits on your board."

"Ms. James, if this is your attempt at a veiled threat, we do not answer to the board about decisions involving students' continued enrollment."

"It was not a veiled threat at all. Simply informing you that both my son and I were completely knowledgeable of the rules of conduct before I enrolled him there." I rubbed my temple, wondering for the umpteenth time did I make the right decision placing Ryder in this exclusive private school with all their rules. He'd been skipped from the fourth to the sixth grade at the end of the last school year and had had adjustment issues since he started Oak Ivy Prep for middle school.

"I'll be there this afternoon once school dismisses."

"I need to check with Mrs. Nelson—"

"You called as if it was an emergency, telling my paralegal to interrupt me while I'm working on an important case, so I'll be there this afternoon for 3:30. If it could wait, then you could have left me a message. I can meet with either you or Mrs. Nelson this afternoon, your choice. Thank you and goodbye." I hung up before my temper really got the best of me. I sent Ryder a text.

Do not go to baseball practice. Wait for me. I have a conference with Ms. Nelson about your behavior.

I waited for his response, knowing that he would check his messages though his phone was supposed to be in his locker. I'd already told him that I needed him to keep it on him at all times in case of emergencies. With all the craziness in the world, especially school shootings, I didn't care about the rules. My son always needed his phone on him. All I had was Ryder. With my entire family scattered throughout the world, he was all I had. Until recently, I also had Raini. Now, she had her own family with Tre and his daughter, Tracie. If anything ever happened to Ryder, I would blame myself.

He responded. *I didn't do anything wrong. I need to go to practice if I'm going to try out for pitcher.*

My son could and would go back and forth with me all day. So, I simply texted, *I don't care. Wait for me in front of the school at 3:15.*

※

I WALKED AHEAD OF RYDER, WHO DRAGGED HIS FEET BEHIND him, still mad Ms. Nelson had reported his behavior in school. "You don't have time to be a comedian in the class. And going back and forth with her like you and I do in front of the class is unacceptable."

He quickened his steps. "Mama, you told me when something isn't right, I should stand up for myself."

"Yes, son, but I also said you can catch more flies with honey than lemon in the manner you talk to people. Especially at this school."

Ryder pushed the front door and held it open for me. "I wasn't wrong, Mama."

Moving through the door, I explained, "There's a time and place for everything. Adults don't like to be challenged by children, even when they're wrong. It can and will be perceived as disrespect. I—"

He stopped walking and huffed impatiently. "Can I go to practice now?"

I turned around quickly to admonish, "Don't cut me off while I'm speaking. You're lucky I don't pull you from the team."

His nostrils flared slightly. "Sorry."

I continued, my voice still elevated. "Yes, I told you to speak your mind or intervene if you see someone smaller than you who is being mistreated or hurt. Not because you disagree with your teacher."

Ryder protested, "It is *mistreatment* of the truth if she's teaching us wrong information. She said that once women were appointed to the Supreme Court there were always two women at any given time. I simply reminded her about the period when Justice O'Connor left, and RBG was the only woman until Justice Sotomayor joined the Supreme Court. That's a simple fact that she shouldn't have gotten wrong, Mama."

"Can you say 'Justice Ginsberg' when discussing her in class? Everyone doesn't know her nickname." Sometimes he was way too smart for his own good. I sighed, "Ry, the next time your teacher presents misinformation, let me know and I can discuss it with her, okay?"

"But, Mama, you can't always be there to solve my problems."

"Trust, I know that, but in this situation, let me handle it."

"That's not fair. I thought you chose this school because I would be able to express myself. If I need to keep my mouth shut, I could've gone to Clayton Middle." Most of his friends from his elementary school were matriculating there after fifth grade. We had a huge battle when I decided he should attend Oak Ivy Prep instead of Clayton for middle school.

"Ryder, enough." I glared at him. "Do you understand that if I have to come up to this school because of your mouth one more damn time, baseball is done?"

He stared back almost insolently. Maybe Dr. Bennett had a point.

"Do...you...understand?"

His gaze dropped. "Yes, ma'am."

I pulled my purse strap back on my arm. "Tee Rain is coming to pick you up after practice and keep you until I come pick you up. I have to work late now because of your little stunt."

He looked at me, relief on his face that I was still allowing him to go to practice. "It wasn't a stunt, Mama. I can't stand that lady and she hates me. Can you switch me to another class?"

"You're in the gifted program. If you switch you'll be in a regular class."

"I don't care about that. I don't need to prove to anyone I'm smart."

"I do care. It's not about proving to anyone that you're smart. You are meant for great things in this life. Not only are you already a grade level above, you're at the top of your class. We will not let that teacher take you away from your purpose." I poked his forehead. "Remember, no one can ever take this from you. I'm raising my son to be well-traveled, well-read, well-spoken, and..."

"Well-rounded," Ryder finished with an eye roll. "I know that, Mama, and I need to go to practice so I can be well-rounded at academics and sports." He smirked, looking like his father. In a rare show of affection in public, he kissed my cheek and hugged me. "Don't worry about me. I'm going to make you proud."

"You better." I smiled, rubbing his head that now came right under my chin, squeezing him tight since he was allowing me to show affection in public.

I CHOSE A STOOL AT THE EDGE OF THE BAR NEXT TO THE WALL at Vincent's, dropped my large leather satchel on the stool next to me, not wanting anyone to strike up a conversation with me. I ordered a whiskey sour, hating that ever since Devin came back into my life, I felt a general unease, constantly wondering if I'd made a mistake not telling him about Ryder. It didn't help that my son had reached a new developmental phase and needed the firm hand of a man.

My son had seen my crazy side when he didn't listen and rarely tried to play me, but I worried that there might be a time when I couldn't corral him when I needed. Sometimes it was too damn exhausting being both mother and father and then trying to excel in my career. Whoever said women can have it all lied. I'd been so distracted with worried thoughts about Ryder after the phone call with Dr. Bennett, I'd fucked up big time at work and missed a vital piece of information that could leave my client with prison time for tax evasion. Hoping to rectify my mistake, I'd remained at the office until security had to lock the building.

I stirred the ice in my whiskey sour, feeling resentful that I couldn't put all the energy I needed to repair the damage to his case, with a son having challenges at school. I wouldn't make partner at this rate.

"Isn't this sort of how we met?" a deep husky voice whispered near my ear.

I screwed my eyes tight that the object of my obsessive thoughts, who could either make my life heaven or hell, had picked up my bag, sat down, and placed it back on his lap. "Not tonight, Devin."

"If not tonight, then when? It's been months since we ran into each other at the French Market and a couple of weeks since I saw you at Deaux's."

Not wanting to be tempted by the devil himself, I barely glanced at him, though I noted that his gray slacks and black sweater fit his body perfectly. Of all the restaurants and bars in New Orleans, how did we end up at the same one?

"Are you following me or something? We've both been in the same city, same career for years, and now I keep bumping into you."

I caught a whiff of his cologne as he perched on the stool next to me, and I had to will myself not to close my eyes again in want. Damn him. Why did he always have to smell so fucking good?

"I like to think of it as fate. That maybe it's time for us."

Refusing to look at him, I downed my drink and reached for my bag.

Devin grabbed my wrist. When I tried to pull away, he held firmly. "I want a drink. You could use another one. I'm buying."

Aggravated at myself that his touch still affected me, I

snapped, "I don't need another drink, and if I did, I would buy it myself."

He let go of my wrist. "Whoa. I'm fairly sure I haven't done anything to have so much anger directed toward me." He looked around the restaurant. "You over here alone, hunched over your drink like someone stole something from you. Is your man here with another woman? Where is he? Do I need to kick his ass?"

I finally met his brown eyes, which glinted with humor.

Reluctantly, I smiled. "Ha. Ha. You have jokes. Besides, I would kick his ass myself."

Devin chuckled. "In that black dress and high-heeled boots, looking like a sexy villain in a comic book? No doubt." He must have communicated telepathically to the bartender because two whiskey sours were placed in front of us.

I pointed at him. "Stop trying to get me drunk so you can have your way with me."

He raised an eyebrow. "Whenever we make love again, I want you alert. No blaming it on the alcohol."

"When we make love again?" I scoffed though my sex dripped at his words. "That's not going to happen."

"Why do you keep fighting the inevitable?" His lips curved before he sipped on his drink. He propped his elbow on the bar to rest his head on his hand as he watched me, somehow making this chance public encounter intimate. He'd aged well, his hair perfectly faded, with natural waves that other men would envy. He used to have a goatee and a mustache but now he had a full groomed beard that I wanted to tug. Only the tiniest of lines around his eyes when he smiled showed his age. "What happened at work?"

"How do you know it's work?"

"If it's not a man, then for you, I'm guessing it's about work. I might be able to help."

I waved my hand dismissively. "I had a long day. Hell, a long week. A case is giving me the blues, and I really don't want to get into all that with you. I'm trying to forget about it until tomorrow."

"Okay, let's talk about anything you want or nothing. Just be my company until I finish my drink."

"Don't you mean once I finish my drink?"

"Royalty, I'm not stupid. If I recall correctly, you can outdrink me. You'll just gulp that whiskey sour down and leave because you're afraid to fall for me again."

"I never fell for you. It was just sex."

While finishing a sip, Devin nodded. "I thought so too, but this attitude you've been giving me since we ran into each other again tells me your feelings were stronger. If I meant nothing to you, you would already be in my bed. You still tremble whenever I'm near."

I hopped off the stool. "As usual, your arrogant ass thinks every woman wants you."

Devin quickly pulled out his wallet. "Wait...

I grabbed my jacket and my purse and headed into the cold, hoping to get to my car before Devin stopped me. I made it to my white Mercedes GLA and searched frantically for my keys.

"Looking for these." He walked up next to me, dangling my keys like a carrot.

I attempted to snatch the keys but fell into his hard chest as he deftly moved them behind his back. My nipples hardened, and I jumped back immediately. I wanted to reach behind him, but that would bring me back into contact with his still sexy, firm, muscled body. "Give me my keys, Devin."

"No." He walked around my car, opened the driver's door, and slid in the seat. "Shit, Royalty, you sit this close to the steering wheel?"

I stifled my giggle at the way he had to awkwardly bend his tall frame until he adjusted the seat. "Get out of my car, Devin."

He started the ignition. "I need a ride home."

I rubbed my arms against the brisk air. "Catch a Lyft. Or call one of your thirsty women."

"Get in, Royalty." He revved the engine. "I would open the door for you, but I don't trust your ass."

"That makes the two of us," I grumbled, tapping my foot impatiently, nervously. My senses were too weak to be this close to him. "Where's your car?"

"At my office, down the street. On nice nights, I walk down here sometimes to grab dinner, watch a game."

"Well then walk your happy behind back. I'm not taking you home."

He closed the door, lowered the window, and peered at me with his irresistible pearly white smile. "Come on, Frosty."

I stomped to the other side and plopped down in the passenger seat. "Only to your office."

Once I buckled up, Devin confidently pulled into the street. "Nice ride."

I grudgingly responded, "I like her. I spend way too much money each month to not drive it as much as I would like."

"Means you work way too hard."

"I have no choice. I'm trying to make partner."

"Why work your ass off for that stuffy firm when you can open your own?"

I rolled my eyes. "All of us don't have your money or influence."

"Then work for me and you would already be considered for partner in six months, tops. We could use someone with your intelligence and ambition."

"You as my boss? With my mouth and yours, you would fire me the first day." I huffed. "No, indeed."

He laughed loudly. "There's that New Orleans talk. I was beginning to think being in DC changed you. Sounding all proper and shit."

"I've been back for years, Devin."

"You should've hit me up."

"Once I moved back, I heard you were married. I'm sure your wife would have loved that."

He winked. "Yep. We would've all met up for beignets and coffee."

I rolled my eyes, enjoying his presence though reluctant to admit it. "Devin, you do know we passed your office?"

"Glad you noticed. I told you I need a ride home."

"And I told you I'm not taking you home."

"You're not. I'm driving."

I crossed my arms. "I'm not sleeping with you."

"Your mind in the gutter, not mine."

"Whatever." I gestured toward my body. "You're hoping to get some of this."

"Not at all."

Silently, I stared at his handsome side profile, lit by the passing streetlights.

Still focused on the road, he conceded with a smile. "After the day you obviously had, you might need some of me. Take the edge off. Make your day better. I could be your early Valentine's gift."

I had to resist the urge to cross my legs at the pulsing in my pussy. "The last thing I need is to get caught back up into you. Not happening."

Devin glanced at me. "Real talk. I wanted a moment of your time. I thought I would get it back at the bar, but you ran out on me. Purely luck that you left your keys. This is the only way I knew I could get your undivided attention. You won't take my calls or return the messages I leave for you at your office. You never even acknowledged the roses I personally handpicked and sent to your office after Deaux's dedication."

Relaxing my arms at the memory of how I felt when I saw the breathtaking bouquet of purple roses that awaited me on my desk, I said softly, "Thank you. They were beautiful."

"I want to know you again. It's been years and you still affect me deeply."

"Devin, we screwed around. We were a summer fling."

"I've never had a problem with getting women. I didn't have

to keep flying almost every weekend to see you for four months just for sex. And the way you been dodging me, it was more than sex for you, too."

I stared ahead through the windshield, mulling his words. Devin had been more than sex for me, even before I knew I carried his baby.

He announced, "I'm divorced with no children. No girlfriend. No dog, only because I'm too busy to give her the care and attention she would need. Own my home, two cars, excellent credit, and have my own firm of four lawyers and two paralegals. We represent the disadvantaged and working class. What's your story?"

Tapping the console between us, I answered, "Work and a man at home. That's it." Guilt plagued me that I couldn't say the man at home was his ten-year-old son.

He shot me a look. "You're not married, especially to that dude I saw you with. He's not your type, and you're the type of woman who would wear her husband's expensive ring proudly."

I arched a brow. "I didn't say husband. I've never been married. Besides, you don't know me enough to know the type of man I like."

"He's not me."

"And that's exactly why I'm with him."

"If you were mine, you wouldn't entertain the thought of another man."

"I don't think about your arrogant ass, Devin."

He contradicted, "No, you hate that you think about me, that you can't get me out of your mind. All I have to do is kiss you and it's over."

To stop the insanity that was threatening to happen if he did kiss me, I hit the console between us. "I'm not you. I don't cheat and break people's hearts. And I need to get home to him."

He abruptly pulled to the side of the road, and I clutched the door handle as the blaring of loud horns and screeching brakes screamed at us.

He shifted in his seat to face me. "Cut the bullshit."

"What the fuck are you doing? Are you trying to kill me?" I yelled.

"I didn't break your heart, you ended us. I don't know what you heard about me since you've been home, but whatever you heard, I'm not that man anymore." Eyes flashing, he accused, "You may have a man, but he's not waiting for you at home. If you don't want me anymore, just say it. You don't have to keep these lies going."

"Good. I don't—" He caught my bold-faced lie with his tongue. He cupped my face with his hands as he licked my lips before he delved deeper in my mouth, coaxing my betraying tongue to respond to his.

Devin gave me another lingering kiss that spoke of things left unsaid, before he pulled back to look at me, his brown eyes heavy with desire. "You still want me."

I whispered, "I hate you."

He studied my expression, his hands still curved to my cheeks. "I hate you, too." He then entwined our fingers together and used one hand to drive the rest of the trip to his home. I loved the touch of his smooth palm against mine and wondered if I was ready for what it meant to be with him again. We were older and both single. I just had to gather the strength to tell him that I was the mother of his only child.

When we pulled into the long, pebbled driveway of his modern, lovely, two-story brick home in the exclusive country club community of English Turn, he kept the engine running. Devin lifted our still clasped hands and kissed the back of my hand. "Come get on this side so you can drive home." He then slid out of the car and stood outside of the door waiting for me.

Knowing he would be going into that beautiful home alone, I was this close to demanding he fuck me after that kiss he planted on my lips. I managed to maneuver across the console to settle myself in the driver's seat, unwilling to be tempted any further by getting out of the car. I felt his deep, hearty laugh through my body.

With a warm and genuine smile, he closed the door, and I pressed the window down. "Look, I know my limitations."

Devin bent to brush my lips with his. "You're obviously not ready for me yet. You have my number, and you know where I live now. When you're ready, come see me." He then walked to his front door without looking back.

I watched him, surprised that he didn't try to pressure me for sex. Then again, he never had to. I'd always been willing to do whatever he wanted with no provocation when we met.

4
ROYALTY

Eleven years ago, Washington, DC

Adjusting my cold shoulder red sweater, I surveyed the bar area where I'd just lost a bet with my girls. "I thought there would be more hotties tonight with that Black Lawyers Association convention in town. Such a waste of my stilettos and outfit, especially because I don't have money for laundry."

Sheena, my roommate, complained, "I told you we should've hung out at Adams Morgan. That's where the money is."

Patrika chimed in. "There are plenty of attractive men here tonight, you're too picky."

Zora added, "Says the woman who's practically engaged."

I wagged my finger in Patrika's face. "Not trying to hear anything from you. Kane can't seem to think without you."

Patrika protested weakly, "I keep trying to get rid of him, but he doesn't go anywhere."

Zora threw her arm around her best friend's shoulders. "And you know you adore him."

Sipping on the rest of my scotch on ice, I scanned the bar and restaurant again. "Back to me, attention back to me. I lost the game, but I don't see anyone in here who seems to be unattached."

Zora quirked a brow. "I'm upping the ante. Instead of asking anyone who you find hot, you have to ask the next man who walks through that door for a date."

Scrunching my nose, I argued, "Anyone? What if he's butt-ass ugly?"

"It's just a date and not a marriage proposal. The dude may turn you down anyway."

I tossed down my drink. "No man has ever turned me down. Fuck it, the next guy who walks through that door."

Patrika laughed. "Hope he's old enough to be your grandfather trying to relive his youth."

"Well, at least I'll have a date."

At that moment, a group of laughing, young, handsome black men in various business casual attire walked into the restaurant.

"Are you freaking kidding me? Every single one of them is hot. You get to choose out of them?" Zora lamented.

"I'll do you one better." I stepped off my stool, smoothed back my sleek long ponytail, and sauntered purposely to the group of four.

When I got closer to them, another cutie walked through the door and my knees almost buckled. Damn, he was one sexy man. Just my type with his ebony skin, low cut fade, groomed mustache and goatee, muscular physique visible in a blue sweater, and tall enough for my five-inch heels. He opened his mouth to say something to his friends before our eyes met.

Bingo.

Unabashedly staring at him, I addressed his group. "Good evening, wondering if you gentlemen would like to join me and my gorgeous friends over there for drinks."

Four heads turned toward the bar and my friends, who were varying shades of black and beautiful waving at the men. Without further conversation, they happily headed to the bar. Except one.

The tall, dark, and handsome object of my attention grabbed my hand before I could follow. "Hey, hey...you're mine for the night."

I smiled. "Yours for the night?"

"Yes. Mine."

"What if I have my eye on one of your friends?"

He shook his head. "Impossible. In fact..." Still holding my hand, he pulled me to the hostess stand. "Table for two."

I looked back at my girls who appeared to be enjoying the company of the men. Only Zora screwed up her face and flicked out her tongue. I gave her the middle finger and then turned back to the sexy stranger. "Can I at least find out your name if I'm supposed to be yours tonight?"

He grinned, his teeth so pearly white I wanted the number to his dentist. "Maybe."

"Then, maybe, I don't want to be alone with you."

He countered in a deep voice. "Yet you haven't let go of my hand."

"I didn't want to hurt your feelings."

Dropping my hand, he grimaced. "Ooh, that hurt."

Surprisingly, already missing the warmth of his palm, I responded, "I think you can take it."

Flirtatiously he quipped, "Yes, I'm sure I can."

The hostess then asked us to follow her to a booth. Although I sat and expected him to sit across from me, he gestured with his head for me to move over. With any other guy, I would've been annoyed at his rather assuming behavior, but I strangely wanted to be near him.

"Order whatever you like." He pointed at the menus that the pretty hostess who lingered a little too long at our table gave him.

The handsome stranger shifted his body toward me with his arm tossed casually behind me on the booth. He even smelled good.

I twisted my body slightly to face him, enjoying our easy, natural chemistry. "We were meant to meet tonight."

"Really? Tell me why?"

"You walked in right when I'd lost a stupid drinking game. The loser had to ask the next person who walked through the door for a date."

I could see my reflection in his brown eyes as he asked, "So not because it was love at first sight?"

"Well, aren't you forward?"

"When it comes to something I want." His gaze lingered on my mouth. "Admit it was love at first sight."

"Not a believer in love at first sight. Maybe like or lust. Besides, you don't even know my name."

"Doesn't matter. When you smiled at me with those damn kissable lips of yours, that was enough."

To stop from grinning like an idiot from his smooth talk, I bit my lip. "You are charming."

"I am that."

I clapped once. "Love a man who can brag on himself."

"And I love a woman confident enough to walk up to me and ask me out."

"Well, I didn't quite ask you out. I asked if you and your friends wanted to join us. You took it upon yourself to separate me from the group."

"Was it not your intention to ask me out?"

"I had to choose one of you. Again, you volunteered."

"I let you out of your misery. You couldn't stop staring."

I scoffed. "Excuse me. That would be you who stopped breathing the minute you saw me."

The vibrations of his deep throaty chuckle traveled my body. "You caught that?"

"I'm surprised you admitted it."

Shrugging his broad shoulders, he smiled. "No shame in my game."

"Yes." Pumping my fist halfway in the air, I announced, "Admitting that you're just playing games with me."

"I already enjoy talking to you...you have a quick comeback for everything I say."

"Let the record reflect, you didn't deny that you're toying with me."

Leaning closer, he kissed my neck slowly and deliciously before backing up, watching me. "I might be. Want to play?"

Neck still tingling from the deft touch of his lips, I quietly assessed his handsome features, uncaring that he probably had a woman. He was too fine, well-spoken, charismatic, and—judging from the Cartier watch on his wrist—of means to not have a woman somewhere eager for his attention. Right now, he only had sexy bedroom eyes for me, and my panties had been slick since he grabbed my hand. "I might. Name's Royalty."

Pleased by my response, he raised one thick, dark brow and repeated my name, the pronunciation rolling seductively off his tongue. Then he gave me his. "Devin."

"You really are the devil trying to tempt me, aren't you?"

He grinned. "I said Devin."

"I know."

"Did you eat?"

"Why?"

"Thinking we can better spend our time alone."

"How do I know you're not a Bundy?"

"I'm worth the risk." His eyes never left mine. "My hotel is five minutes away."

"You're visiting?"

"Here for the conference with my boys."

"All lawyers?"

He frowned. "How did you know the conference was for lawyers?"

"I'm just starting law school."

"Georgetown?"

"No, Howard."

He looked impressed. "Can I see your phone?"

I placed it between us.

Devin picked it up. "I'm texting one of your friends that we're about to get out of here and to let my friends reassure them I'm no threat."

"You don't know any of my friends' names." I tried to take it back.

He smoothly moved it right out of my reach. "I'm not checking if you have a man. We're just having fun tonight, right?"

"Yes."

"My guess is one of your most recent texts is to or from one of those lovely ladies at the bar." Devin announced, "Ah...one of them is named Zora, right?"

"Umm...hmm." I couldn't believe I was going to let a perfect stranger take me to his hotel, but the need to have him inside of me wiped away any fears or worries that I was placing myself in a precarious situation. I'd always trusted my instincts and knew two things—one, this man wasn't dangerous, and two, he would change my life.

For better or worse, it didn't matter. I loved taking risks, and he might be my biggest gamble.

THE PASSION, THE HEAT, THE FIRE, THE CHEMISTRY, OR whatever euphemism to describe the incessant need to fuck anytime we were in each other's presence was absolutely insane. From that very first night when we didn't even make it out of the parking lot before he had me screaming his name in the backseat of his luxury rental SUV, we were madly in lust.

I set up residence at Devin's hotel that weekend, studying in between waiting for him to return from the conference. I thought we were only having a weekend fling until he called me a couple of weeks later to say he wanted to see me again.

For the next four months, Devin flew into town every other weekend and helped me study law before he studied me. We eventually talked long enough to know we were both, amazingly, from New Orleans. He was four years older than my twenty-three years, a popular attorney who contemplated running for District Attorney, his dad a well-known local politician in a bid for mayor.

Any time he tried to ask me about my dating life or tried to say anything about his, I would kiss him or grab his dick, momentarily distracting him, unwilling to make our precious time together more than what it was meant to be.

One weekend, a few days before Devin's trip into DC to visit me, while looking in the mirror after taking a shower, my breasts appeared swollen. I touched my nipples and winced in pain. *Shit!* I quickly rushed to my laptop to look up symptoms, and though scared out of my mind to know the truth, I drove to CVS to purchase a pregnancy test.

Devin and I had gotten reckless one of the last times he visited. After a fun night at an illusionist show where we gave each other hand jobs underneath the table, we'd went into the alley behind the theatre. Within seconds he'd had my breasts pressed against the bricks, his hand in my mouth, my dress hiked over my ass, impaling me over and over again with his own magic stick. I'd forgotten to take the morning-after pill, too caught up in him and my studies.

When that strip displayed a plus sign, my temples began to throb while I sifted through my emotions about my future, about being a single mother, what my parents would think, and would I be able to finish school. The one prevailing thought was that I needed to finally know more about the father of my baby. Cross-legged on my sofa, I scoured the internet and social media looking for anything related to Devin Toussaint. At first, I saw nothing but his financial contributions to campaigns, his political positions on different topics, pictures with his parents and friends. Even saw an old pic of him with Tre LaSalle, a guy

I went to high school with and my best friend Raini's old crush.

I didn't see any pics of women who appeared to be significant in his life and exhaled, thinking that maybe he didn't have anyone serious. He had seemed to be really into me, beyond our physical connection, texting encouraging words when I had an exam or paper and checking on me when we weren't together. We were from the same city, we'd chosen the same profession, and I missed him terribly when he wasn't with me. Maybe we could be more. Maybe we could be a family.

He'd always taken time out of his busy schedule to fly to see me, though I'd never asked or required it of him. Maybe it was time for me to suggest a trip home to spend time with him. I didn't travel back and forth to New Orleans often since the only person who lived in New Orleans now was Raini, my best friend. But if Devin and I were going to be in a real relationship, I would visit home more.

My cell alerted me to a text. I smiled when I saw Devin's name.

Sorry, Queen. Unexpected change in my schedule. I can only stay until Sun morning. Check yourself in to the Waldorf and be wearing that red lace I bought you last time. Be wet and ready...inside you by nine. TTYL

This wasn't the first time he made last-minute changes. I studied his text, my gut telling me that I needed to do another search. Words I hadn't been able to type.

Stomach tied in knots, I typed in "Devin Toussaint's wife" and hit enter with bated breath.

A feeling I could only describe as grief flowed through me. Loss of hope, of happiness, and a future with a man I'd only admitted to myself I'd already loved. The wedding announcement stated that the happy couple were married in a lovely ceremony in a New Orleans mansion ten months ago. The blushing bride, Nia Winston Saint, was a teacher and the daughter of a Congressman. They made a young, gorgeous, and powerful couple. I stared at his beautiful petite wife who probably had no idea that within the first year of her marriage, her husband had already strayed. He had been with me for almost four months. *And now I'm pregnant with his child.* Willing myself not to cry, I picked up my cell.

Don't bother coming here again. It's over.

Devin immediately called me, and I sent him to voicemail. He called multiple times that day, sent me texts begging me to answer the phone and talk to him. Asking to talk in person, trying to understand my change of heart.

He called me off and on for the next three months, and I refused to answer. I knew if I answered I would tell him I was pregnant, and I didn't have the strength to handle it if he rejected me and denied our child. Truthfully, I was more afraid that if Devin accepted my pregnancy and wanted to continue seeing me, I would have gone against everything I believed.

I'd fallen helplessly, hopelessly, unequivocally in love with him.

5

ROYALTY

"What do you think about this dress?" I asked, twirling the bottom of the tulle dress in the full-length mirror. Without Raini's knowledge I'd called the bridal shop and asked them to send other dresses in the same color scheme and by the designer of the original one Raini had chosen for her maid of honor. I figured I would ask for forgiveness rather than permission.

Raini and I were at her and Tre's home for our last fitting, with her wedding to take place in two weeks. We were in one of their guest rooms with the seamstress who'd signed a non-disclosure agreement since Mrs. LaSalle wanted Raini's wedding and reception gowns kept a secret until the wedding day.

"We are not changing your dress at the last minute, Royalty. I thought you loved the one I chose. Besides, I do not want Mrs. LaSalle's panties in a bunch. She has been getting on my nerves with how everything is supposed to be. She helped me choose the gowns, and it's the one thing we agreed on."

"Mrs. LaSalle does have good taste, and I do like the design, but I think I want to wear this one instead of that strapless. It's the same pattern, and besides, as the future Mrs. LaSalle, you can afford to get this one and have it altered in time."

It had been a week since Devin kissed me and all those erotic moments we had shared in the past came rushing back in my mind tenfold, haunting me in my bed at night. I didn't even want Anthony to touch me, so I'd made excuses for why I didn't want to go out on Valentine's Day.

She moved closer to me, playfully tracing the top of the deep V in my pink glitter bodice, which displayed the brown skin between my breasts. "This smile on your face, wanting to wear a sexier dress, is about Devin, isn't it?"

I'd told her about the roses but not about our kiss.

"No...well, kind of...I don't know why I'm still crazy about him, knowing he had a new wife while sexing me. And now that he's divorced and trying to get with me, it's starting to consume my thoughts."

"Starting? You've been obsessing about him ever since he came back into your life. Even messing around with poor Anthony to avoid dealing with him. You really should stop seeing him when you know you want Devin."

"And I keep telling you that Anthony and I have an understanding. We're not in a relationship. We see each other when we do. Even Ryder doesn't know we've been dating. He thinks he's one of my colleagues." Shrugging, I turned back to the mirror, straightening the bodice.

Raini stood behind me. "Ryder is smarter than you give him credit for. You invited Anthony to the dedication."

"No...no, he invited himself because he wanted to go. I asked him to meet me there. See, if we talked more often you would know these things." I turned to face her and smiled. "Like, you would know that last Friday I bumped into Devin at Vincent's, and he feigned some excuse so I could bring him home. He lives in this bad-ass house in English Turn."

Her eyes widened. "You had sex with Devin and didn't tell me?"

I glanced at the seamstress, who had stepped into the hall to make a call. "Hush, now who's the loud one? People do know him."

Rolling her eyes almost to the back of her head, she spoke in a lower tone, "What happened?"

"Nothing. He kissed me, told me that now that I know where he lives, I'm welcome to stop by anytime."

She squinted her eyes and pointed at me. "Royalty, all you did was kiss? Not seeing him for years and all that pent-up passion and your fast tail only kissed? Heifer, you are lying. That was the night you texted if Ryder could stay overnight, and you didn't pick him up until Saturday morning."

"Hey, I needed some time to myself to digest this new Devin. Besides, I do know how to control myself, unlike you, who gave Tre all your goodies before you even had your first date."

"Umm...smart ass, that would be you and Devin...oh about eleven years ago."

I'd finally confided in Raini about how Devin and I met, and how I found out that he had a wife the same day my pregnancy test screamed "positive" with his child.

"Touché." I checked myself out in the mirror again. "It is weird, right? He could tell I wanted him, but he didn't pressure me or even invite me inside. Said something like, I wasn't ready for him yet."

Raini nodded. "Because you're not."

"How can I be ready for a man I'm not sure I can trust?" I looked back at Raini, who'd already changed back into her clothes. "He has been really sweet and sent me diamond earrings and Godiva chocolate on Valentine's, and one rose every day at work since I saw him because he still doesn't have my personal number or address."

She peered at my ears and smiled. "These are exquisite, Royalty. He has good taste. Diamond earrings and chocolates to your job... Devin is courting you."

I twisted my lips to hide my smile. "Courting sounds so old-fashioned."

"Devin could easily get your personal number and home address if he wanted to, so yes, he's courting you, taking his time with you." Raini moved around me to unzip. "You look gorgeous in this dress and it's actually more you than the one we chose."

I turned around to hug her. "Thank you!"

"I guess I can tell you now that he and his family were invited to the wedding, since you're already dressing with him in mind."

Ignoring the flutter in my stomach at the thought of seeing him again in such a romantic setting, I asked, "How in the world did that happen? The Toussaints and the LaSalles hate each other."

"Although Tre and Devin had stopped speaking, the families were still close until Tre decided to run against Mr. Toussaint for Mayor. Before that, the families were friends, which is how Tre and Devin know each other. Tre's mother is using this wedding as an olive branch, and they've accepted."

"Well, it's a good thing the only child at the wedding will be Tracie and Ryder will be at a baseball camp that weekend. I couldn't handle telling Devin about Ryder right before your wedding."

Raini sat down in the Victorian chair in her guest room, watching me change back into my jeans and T-shirt. "Royalty, you're only avoiding Devin because of Ryder. What do you think Devin is going to do once he finds out?"

I answered without thought. "Hate me. Take away my son."

"Or he loves you and Ryder gets a father. He needs his father."

"We don't know what kind of father Devin will be. What if he's horrible and Ryder is better off not knowing him?" It was an excuse I'd used over the years to justify my decision.

"He could be the worst father ever, but every human wants to know their people. My mother is practically non-existent in my life. I only invited her to my wedding out of courtesy, but at least I can say I know her. Do you honestly think he would be a horrible father?"

I groaned. "No...probably not. If his social media is any indication, he seems to care about children. His firm does a lot of philanthropic activities geared toward schools and children. I guess I can't shake the fear he would hate me for keeping Ryder a secret for so long. I don't want him to hate me," I admitted softly.

She rushed to my side and wrapped her arms around me. "Aww...Royalty, you love him, don't you?"

I finally said my truth out loud. "Yes. I've always loved him. I hate it that no man has ever compared to him."

Raini squeezed tighter. "If I can have a happy ending with my first love, so can you. You have to stop running from him."

"I want to, but then I get scared again, and I hate being this person."

"Then don't be. You kept encouraging me to tell Tre the truth about my father's past, and I almost lost him because I didn't."

I countered, "You didn't almost lose him. He wanted to be there for you, and you were too scared that you'd ruined his career. He used your time apart to prove his love for you by clearing Deaux's name. But my secret is more personal, and now that Devin's back in my life, I'm afraid to lose him again."

"Why didn't you tell me about Devin? Why did you keep that a secret from me?"

"I was embarrassed, Raini. You know I pride myself on not being caught up in foolishness with a man, and he got me good. Not only messing around with a married man, but then getting knocked up by him. My parents hold marriage to a high standard, and they would've judged me for sleeping with a married man. Bad enough my mother told me I was on my own when I told her I was pregnant. She told me if I was grown enough to have unprotected sex, I was grown enough to raise my child. I tried to make it work in D.C. after graduation, but my friends and roommate who were also in graduate school could only help so much. I felt like a failure when I had to come back here. You think I wanted to come back to the very city where the chances of running into Devin and his wife were high?"

She looked at me. "You just did what you needed to do to take care of Ryder. You needed my help, and I needed a family."

I nodded, wiping my eyes. "I managed to avoid him all these years by not attending any social networking events or conventions involving lawyers, always looking over my shoulder, until he took an interest in you."

Raini sighed exasperatedly. "For the millionth time, I'm sure he was attracted, but we connected because we were both from New Orleans and happened to be in New York at the same time. Once he saw you again, I didn't exist. Even Pierre noticed, remember? You can't possibly believe he likes me after all this time?"

"No, I don't anymore. Thinking it might just be fate." I had decided to visit Raini when she used to show her work at the French Market next to Pierre, another artist, and Devin had been there buying one of her paintings. I wanted to run far away when I realized that the person who had been flirting with her happened to be the love of my life and the father of my child.

"Mama Rain, are you here?" Tracie called from the front of the house, interrupting our conversation. "Daddy was rushing me again at the museum saying he needed to come back so we could all have dinner."

"You've been to the children's museum countless times, and I was hungry." Tre's commanding voice trailed his daughter's.

"We could've had a snack at the museum," she accused, "You just missed Mama Rain."

He retorted, "So, you missed her too."

We both shook our heads, laughing at their lively banter as Tracie knocked and burst through the door a second later.

Raini scolded warmly, "How many times do we have to tell you to knock and wait until you receive permission to come in?"

Tracie, Tre's nine-year-old daughter, soft hair in thin cornrows, ran straight toward Raini, who opened her arms wide. "Sorry, I keep forgetting."

"Which is why we keep our bedroom door locked." Tre came in, positive energy flooding the room as he kissed me on the cheek. "How are you, sis? Where's little man?"

"I'm good, big bro. Baseball camp with his school for the weekend."

Tracie hugged me around my waist. "Are you eating dinner with us?"

A wave of loneliness assailed me as I watched the happy family and at the thought of going to an empty home since Ryder wasn't there. "I...I actually have other plans."

Raini leaned against Tre's side. "I hope it's with a certain someone."

"I hope so, too."

Tre looked at Raini and me. "Do I want to know who this person is?"

Laughing, we both answered, "Nope."

※

TAKING A DEEP BREATH, I PRESSED HIS DOORBELL, HOLDING his dry-cleaned plastic-wrapped suit jacket in my hand. When Devin opened the door only wearing blue basketball shorts, my mouth watered like he was a slowly cooked rib-eye. My gaze assessed him from top to bottom. His beautiful ebony skin, his still taut abs, the fine hairs across his pecs, his belly button so damn sexy, and the faint imprint of the most pleasure-giving part of his body.

"Eyes up here," he teased.

Straightening my shoulders, never shirking from complimenting a handsome man, I said, "I can acknowledge that your body is still banging since you're intent on showing it off."

"Showing it off? You stopped by unannounced, and it's after eight on a Saturday night. I don't lounge fully dressed."

"I'm surprised you're not out. It's still early. Unless I interrupted something."

He stepped outside the door in his bare feet. "How did you get through security?"

"I'm good with numbers. I remembered the code you used."

"How is that possible? I didn't even think you were paying that much attention."

"I'm a genius with numbers, my line name in my sorority is Rain Man."

Devin cracked a smile. "What do I owe the honor of your very sexy presence?"

I touched one of my diamond earrings. "To thank you for these and to return this." I extended the jacket.

He folded his arms over his bare chest and ignored my outstretched hand. "You could have had it delivered to my office or brought it to me over there. Why bring it tonight to my home unannounced?" His grin widened. "You're trying to see if I have a woman?"

Shaking my head, I protested, "I don't care whose heart you're breaking now. One of my colleagues doesn't live far from here, and I had a meeting with him. This jacket has been in my car for almost a month. I forgot to give it to you when you *made* me take you home. Take your jacket, please." He didn't have to know my colleague was a woman by the name of Raini who lived a half hour away.

He looked me up and down with a frown. "'Him'? You had a meeting with a man on a Saturday wearing those ass-hugging jeans and that see-through T-shirt?"

I glanced down at my shirt. "My shirt isn't see-through."

"Then why do I know your nipples are dark?"

"Because you already..." I stopped talking when I noticed the twinkle in his dark brown eyes.

Devin's hand closed around my hand holding the jacket and pulled me inside.

6

DEVIN

Royalty stood awkwardly in my foyer, unsure what to do next. As much as I wanted her, especially how her sleek ponytail emphasized her cheekbones and pouty lips, and the way her jeans and T-shirt curved her B cups and her fine ass, I needed to take us slow this time.

I did my best to keep my eyes focused on her face, not wanting my shorts to do a noticeable tentpole. I sensed her nervousness underneath her bravado, that she was affected by me. I let go of her hand long enough to place my jacket in my hall closet.

"I was just watching the Pelicans game, eating pizza. I remember how much you liked sports. Join me."

Allowing me to pull her in the direction of my media room, she spoke, "I'm surprised you don't have season tickets since they're playing here tonight."

I looked back at her, enjoying the feel of her hand in mine. "I do have season tickets...didn't feel like going anywhere. My cousin and one of his friends are using the tickets tonight." We walked through the living area and stepped down into the media room where my large meat lover's pizza and beer rested. "You want something to drink? I have water, apple juice, tea, and if you want a stronger drink, I have a full bar on my deck."

She let go of my hand, mouth agape at my one-hundred-inch flat screen and the eight-seater theatre. "This is the life. I wouldn't go to a game either if I had this room." She dropped in my leather recliner and picked up my beer, all apparent nervousness gone. "You might as well grab you another."

"You're sitting in my chair."

She waved her hand away. "There are several chairs in this room. I'm a guest." She picked up a slice of pizza and took a bite over the box.

"I can get you a plate or napkin," I said wryly.

"No...it's just us. We can eat over the box. Grab us a few more beers and napkins." Royalty began yelling at the TV. "That was a fucked-up call, are you blind?"

"Do you want anything else, madam?" I asked, standing almost in front of her to get her attention. She had become that focused on the game.

She perused my body slowly, resting briefly on my dick, before making it up to my knowing smirk. "Can you put a shirt on please?"

I chuckled rubbing my abs. "Too tempting?"

"No. You just made yourself look thirsty since I'm not interested." She giggled at her own joke before she took a large gulp of beer from the bottle, inserting her tongue briefly in the top, causing my nature to rise. *Down, boy.*

"You really should work for my firm...we need lawyers who can lie with a straight face."

I heard her laughter as I headed to my bedroom to put on a shirt.

※

BY THE TIME THE GAME ENDED IT HAD GONE INTO DOUBLE overtime with the Pelicans winning by a basket. The pizza and beer were long gone, the bag of Oreos I offered as dessert completely devoured. Royalty had positioned the recliner to lie flat and her eyes were closed now that the excitement of the game had waned.

I poked her shoulder, waking her up. "Where do you live?"

"Gentilly area."

"It's going to take you at least forty minutes with the construction on the bridge. Besides, it's too late to be driving across the city."

"I drive fast and can be home in twenty minutes. I've gone to parties and driven home later than this."

I grabbed her keys near her bag in the chair next to her and placed them in my pocket. "Tomorrow."

She used the arms of the chair to sit up. "Damn. I got to remember to hold on to my keys when you're around. I can't spend the night out."

"Why, because your man would be upset?"

"Yes."

"You haven't checked your phone once since you've been here. Why aren't you with him anyway on a Saturday night?"

She folded her arms. "He works offshore two weeks on and two weeks off, if you must know. I still need to get home."

"He works offshore, that little man?"

"He's a geologist and your height, he's just slimmer."

I shrugged. "Love that you're comparing us, and I must be winning, or you wouldn't be here tonight."

She scooted to the end of the chair. "Bye, Devin."

I tugged on her hand, stopping her movement. "Come on now, I wouldn't be me if I wasn't confident."

"You mean narcissistic."

"Arrogant, yes...narcissistic, no."

"You have to admit you have narcissistic tendencies."

"The younger me, maybe. Besides, I wasn't that way with you, ever."

She responded rather crossly, "You wanted me on your terms.

You decided when you would come to see me, changing plans at the last minute."

I contradicted, "I would've been there anytime you asked. I took the lead because I had to see you, and you never invited me to D.C. Our relationship wasn't and doesn't have to be on my terms."

She tilted her head, assessing me. "That remains to be seen." She held her hand out for her keys. "I am more than capable of driving home."

"You had two beers and two whiskey sours, and you can't stop yawning. I'm looking out for you."

Royalty collapsed back in the recliner. "Give me a blanket, and I can sleep right here."

I whispered near her ear, "I have a brass waterbed."

"No, you don't. Stop quoting Morris Day." Eyes closing, she turned over in the chair, her plump ass tempting me to cup and squeeze it. Somehow, I'd managed to keep my mind on the game and not how much I really wanted to fuck Royalty until the cops came knocking, we would be so loud. "I'm sleeping right here."

I shook my head and quickly scooped her up in my arms.

"Hey, put me down," she protested weakly. Her head fell against my chest, and she wrapped her arms around my neck.

"Shh...you can have my bedroom. I'll take one of the guest rooms." I cradled her to me as I headed to my master suite. I placed her on my California King, kissed her forehead, and backed away.

She smiled sleepily and stretched on the bed. "A couple more drinks and you could've had your way with me."

"Like I said, I want you fully alert when we make love again."

Royalty met my eyes and deepened her voice, mimicking mine, "'Make love again.' Why are you being all romantic with your words and actions? Sending me flowers every day. Me and you never got down like that. It was just lust between us, mad crazy passion, but still lust. We had fun fuckin', that's all, Devin."

I leaned against the doorjamb, folding my arms, willing my

dick to stay calm at the ease with which she discussed our sexual history while in my bed. "If that's all that was between us, why did you come here and stay with me tonight?"

She draped her eyes with her arm. "You made me spend the night."

"Royalty, no one can make you do anything. Real talk."

"I don't know if I should be here." She kept her eyes covered. "I've been riding around with your suit jacket in my car trying to get the nerve to return it to you. I did have a meeting earlier and didn't want to go to an empty house, so I came here. If you weren't home or with a woman, I would've left your jacket and kept it going. But you were home and alone."

"Why is it so difficult for you to acknowledge that we still have feelings for each other?"

"I like my life. Not sure I want to shake it up."

I grinned. "You used to like adventure."

"I was in my early twenties, didn't know shit about life."

"Yet you're still here."

"I'm a glutton for punishment."

I tapped my heart. "Ooh, now that cut."

She moved her arm and stared at the ceiling. "I'm serious, Devin."

"I am too."

"I've been torturing myself being here tonight with you."

I moved closer. "Then stop. I want to be with you, too."

"I have a man."

"Which we both know is not the man for you or you wouldn't be in my house tempting yourself."

She pushed herself up against the cushion headboard. "And you're the man for me?"

I answered without hesitation. "Yes."

Shaking her head, she yawned and stretched. "Devin, I had a long day. Let me sleep."

Staring at the uncompromising line her mouth now made, I left my bedroom and rested against the wall right outside my door. She'd given me the signs all night, constantly touching my hand, my thigh, my arm. She gave me flirty eyes and a teasing smile every time we looked at each other. She wanted me to take and not ask what she was offering, and as much as I wanted to feel her naked body against mine all night, I had to be different toward her. Different than I had been with other women, different than I had been with her when we first met. I had to be if I wanted her to see me as potential and not just as a good fuck.

Debating whether to jerk off once I made it to the guest room upstairs, I pulled off my shirt and slid under the covers. I hadn't done that in years, never needed to since I always had a woman somewhere willing. Even tonight the woman downstairs would gladly ride me into oblivion. Except I wanted a relationship with her. Tonight had been the most fun I'd had without sex in a long time, and a glimpse of what she and I could be, genuinely enjoying each other's company. Frustrated, I picked up my cell and dialed the number she'd finally given me earlier.

7

ROYALTY

Feigning irritation, I answered, "Why are you calling me when I'm right downstairs?"

"The fact that you're in my bed is fucking with me, and I'm having trouble controlling myself around you. Wouldn't want you doing something you're not ready for."

Needing him to pound me desperately, I lowered my voice, "I never do anything which I'm not prepared and ready for."

Devin warned, "Queen, you know if I come back, hard as I am right now, we're fucking."

I smiled in the darkness. He'd given me that nickname the second time he visited me. "Don't think you calling me Queen is going to make it easy to get in these lace panties."

He groaned. "Please say you have a matching bra and it's red."

"I do and it is, but I don't sleep in my bra."

"Are you naked in my bed?"

"Does wearing only my lace panties count as naked?"

"Why are you playing with me?"

"I'm not, you called me."

"Do you want to feel my dick inside of you again?"

I clicked off the cell, thinking maybe I had gone too far,

looking down at my T-shirt, which I hadn't removed. I needed to keep a level head until I figured what the hell I wanted from him. I had been giving him mixed signals all night. I came here to talk about us and tell him about Ryder, but then I chickened out when he opened the door all yummy and irresistible with that killer smile and dark eyes that gleamed sinful pleasures only he could provide.

I so wanted him between my legs, but I wasn't yet ready to ignite a fire that only he could extinguish. After the fun time I had with him tonight, I wasn't ready to have my heart broken again. I wasn't ready for him to hate me once he found out about Ryder.

Knock. Knock.

I squeezed my legs tight, trying to stop the yearning. "Devin, I'm not having sex with you. So, take your ass back up those stairs and go to sleep."

"Open the door please."

"I'm sleepy. You forced me to spend the night. Let me go to sleep."

"Open the door."

I threatened, "I swear if you're naked on the other side of the door or you kiss me, I'm punching you dead in the face. I'm so serious."

I could hear the smile in his voice. "Open the door, Royalty."

"Umm...I can't get out of bed. I'm not wearing my jeans. The door is unlocked."

I turned on the lamp as he opened the door, back to wearing only his shorts, and he carried a blanket and pillow.

"What are you doing?"

"Sleeping on the floor next to you."

I pulled the covers tighter. "Devin..."

"I'm not trying anything, I swear. I had fun tonight and I just want to be near you in case you decide you never want to see me again."

His sincere sweetness at that moment added another layer to this complex man that I hadn't yet figured out. "Okay."

Watching this Devin, who had been a gentleman, more like a friend this whole evening, spread his blanket so that he could sleep next to me was breaking down all my defenses. I turned off the lamp once he settled down and turned over on my side to face him, and he did likewise. I could barely see his face from the moonlight that dipped in through the skylight in his ceiling.

"Why?"

"Why what?"

"Why aren't you trying to have sex with me?"

"Do you want to have sex with me?"

"You know the answer to that question."

"The problem is, you're not sure of the answer. I want more than just sex with you."

"What if all I want is sex?"

His deep chuckle sent shivers through my body. "Queen, you wouldn't be so conflicted if all you desired is a good time. You're still that sensually open, vibrant woman I met, and I have no qualms about us engaging in a purely sexual relationship if that's all you wanted from me." I suddenly felt his warm large hand around mine. "When I met you, you wouldn't allow me to tell you anything personal about my life, and you only shared some of yourself with me. This time I want us to really get to know one another. Is that okay with you, Queen?"

"Yes." For now, accepting that my life would be forever changed once again by Devin Toussaint, I closed my hand around his and we both drifted off to sleep, sharing our likes and dislikes.

The next morning, with my arm still hung over the downy mattress, Devin and his bedding were gone. Then I noticed the coffee, oatmeal, and toast on a wooden tray next to the bedside lamp. Feeling slightly hung over from drinking and lack of sleep, I slowly placed my legs over the side of the bed and sipped on the coffee. The knock on the door reminded me to cover my body. "Come in."

Dressed in an impeccably tailored dark suit with light blue tie, Devin greeted me with a brilliant smile. "Morning. How did you sleep?"

"I would've slept better if a certain somebody didn't keep me up all night."

"Go back to sleep and stay as long as you like. I should be back before eleven. Would love to have brunch with you."

I took a bite of the wheat toast. "I don't have a change of clothes to go out."

"I can cook. There should be an extra toothbrush and toothpaste in my bathroom. Towels and washcloths are on the sink. Make yourself at home."

Squinting my eyes at the bright sun peeking through the blinds, I asked, "What time is it?"

"Almost eight."

"How are you even up this early when we went to bed so late?" I took a bite of the oatmeal, which contained dried cranberries and brown sugar. "Umm...this is delish." I gobbled down a couple more spoonfuls.

"Thanks, it's my go-to breakfast." Devin grinned. "I'm a night owl and a morning person, which means I rarely get enough sleep. I forgot you sleep so hard. I showered, dressed, and made you breakfast, and you didn't budge."

"Yes, I need all my sleep." I gave an appraising glance at his attire. "You go to church?"

He responded with a straight face. "Yes, I'm a heathen six days out of the week and love the Lord all day Sunday at Greater St. Stephens."

Giggling, I propped myself up higher on my pillows. "That's what Raini says about me."

His smiled widened. "What church?"

"I'm at Franklin Avenue."

"I know the pastor and been meaning to visit." He stepped

back toward the door. "I have a meeting with one of the deacons about fundraisers, otherwise I would miss service today and spend more time with you. Maybe one Sunday I can visit your church. Or you can come with me to mine."

Staring at him in amazement that he seemed sincere in his commitment to church, I commented, "I can't tell you the last time a man invited me to church."

Devin suddenly bent down and pecked me softly on the lips before pleading with his eyes. "Be here when I get back."

I nodded, touching my lips.

Once I heard the door close, I scrambled out of bed to watch him back out of the garage, and continued to watch until I couldn't see his car. I had it bad.

I had to laugh at myself before I padded back to his bathroom and jumped in his glass shower. We would have naughty fun in this large shower meant to share, on days I didn't feel like riding him in the sunken tub. I had a nice renovated four-bedroom home in an older neighborhood that I loved, but his five-bedroom house belonged in a magazine, with its warm and vibrant brown, yellow, and red décor throughout the rooms. No doubt there were definitely women hoping to be his Mrs. so they could live in this home and do what I'm doing right now.

Throwing on his fresh spring-scented fluffy terry cloth robe, I wandered into the gourmet kitchen with my dirty breakfast dishes, deciding to cook him an early Sunday dinner instead of brunch. Surprisingly, he had plenty of food in his pantry and refrigerator.

I'd been pleased that he'd been thoughtful enough to prepare such a hearty breakfast. We always met up in a hotel, and he'd never even seen my apartment, so we'd never cooked for each other. I absolutely loved to cook, and since I didn't have to pick up Ryder until three, I had plenty of time to make roast beef, oven baked potatoes, and string beans.

I HAD JUST TURNED OFF THE STOVE AND IT WAS A LITTLE AFTER eleven when Ryder called.

"Mama?" I could hear the disappointment in his voice. Tryouts were yesterday and the decision whether Ryder made the team and pitcher was announced today.

"Yes, baby. What's wrong?"

"I didn't make pitcher."

"It's okay," I soothed him. "You still on the team, right?"

"They accepted everyone on the team. Only two people can be the pitcher, and I really thought I had it. I didn't even make relief pitcher."

"Oh, Ry...I'm sorry. I know how much you wanted this. There's always next year. Maybe we can get private coaching."

"Can you pick me up? I don't want to be here anymore. We're not doing anything but hanging out. I want to be home with you."

I looked around at the table I'd just set for Devin and I. "Ry, you have to be a good sport and be happy for the rest of the team. Sometimes you don't get what you want, even when you've worked hard for it."

"Mama...please." I could hear his voice cracking. My son rarely cried, even as a baby.

I sighed. Motherhood called. "Okay, give me a few minutes and I'll be on my way."

I retrieved my clothes out of the dryer and took off Devin's robe. I texted him right before I left his home.

I had to go unexpectedly. I used the code to lock up. (Yes, I memorized the code after I saw you input it). Made you Sunday dinner, planned to join you but can't now. See you at the wedding.

☙❧

I ARRIVED AT LAFRENIERE PARK AND CHILDREN WERE laughing and running, enjoying the beautiful cool day. Burgundy shirts that represented Oak Ivy Prep were scattered throughout the area. I remained in the car, searching the grounds until I spotted Ryder walking alone on the trail. I quietly joined him on the path, and I nudged his shoulder when I caught up with him. He looked up, surprised.

"Mama, why didn't you text me? I could've met you at the car."

"Maybe I wanted to take a walk. "

"In those shoes?" He pointed to my heels.

"I'll have you know I can jog in these shoes." And I picked up speed to a slow jog.

He looked around. "Mama, stop, you're embarrassing me."

"Well, you better put a smile on that face or Mama's going to keep jogging, may even start to sprint."

He hurried his footsteps to hug me from the back. "Stop before your hurt yourself."

"Do you really care if I fall, or are you more concerned about me embarrassing you?" I stopped and looked back at him.

"Come on, Mama, I wouldn't ever want anything to happen to you."

I grasped the arms around my waist before he could move them. "Had to check because lately I've been feeling like I don't have my little boy anymore."

Ryder rested his head on my back. "Mama, what did I do wrong? I practiced hard, did what the coach asked of me, and I still didn't get to be pitcher."

"Do you want to play baseball or be a pitcher?"

He responded in a low voice, "Play baseball."

"Well, you still can do that, baby." I patted his arm still around my waist. "We can do our best and sometimes we still don't win, but it doesn't mean we give up. We keep trying. You don't give up when you don't score well on a test, or mess up on one of your video games, do you?"

"No, ma'am."

I pulled him around to look in his face. "Exactly. So, you're going to lift your head up and be proud that you did your best today and strive to be the best player on the team."

He nodded, a slow smile forming.

"What position *are* you playing? I know my Ry is not a bench warmer."

Ryder bragged, "First base."

"What?" I exclaimed and gave him a hug, almost lifting him off his feet. "That's amazing. You have to make sure hitters end up with no runs."

"Mama, put me down," he hissed.

I quickly let him go to ruffle the top of his sponge hairstyle. "Sorry, I keep forgetting you're a young man now."

"I guess it *is* an important position. Coach did say that I had to be ready at all times." He looked around the park. "Can we go home now?"

"Only if you give me that pretty smile of yours."

He rolled his eyes slightly before displaying his even white teeth, so much like his father.

After I checked him out of camp, I asked, "Ry, do you still think about your father?"

"Sometimes."

"Are you okay with it being just you and me?"

"Most days."

"And those other days?"

"I see how happy Tee Rain is with Unc Tre, and I want that for you."

"You wouldn't be jealous? Because when I dated Mr. Isaiah you gave him the blues."

"That's ancient, Mama. I was eight, and I could tell he was only being nice to me because he liked you."

"I want you to meet your father, and I'll do all I can to make sure that happens."

Ryder only shrugged. "It's cool either way."

He suddenly took off running toward the car.

"Ry?" I called, wondering if I upset him bringing up his father.

He slid into the passenger seat and had buckled up by the time I made it to the driver's side.

I plopped down, exhausted, in the car. "Hey, don't run off like that. I really can't run in these shoes."

"Sorry," he mumbled, pulling out his earbuds.

I touched his arm. "I'm sorry if I upset you talking about your father."

"I don't know how I feel. I used to want to meet him, but you always told me it wasn't possible. So, it really doesn't matter. As long as it's me and you, no one else matters, Mama."

Blinking back tears, I continued, "Maybe you need a man in your life."

"I have Unc Tre now, and I still have Grandad and Unc Lee. I don't need any other man, especially not my father, who didn't care enough to want to meet me."

"It's not that he didn't care enough..." My voice trailed off, unsure what to say next.

"I'm almost eleven, Mama. If he wanted to meet me, he would have years ago." He pulled his cap down lower on his head and sank down in his seat. "Can we just go home, please?"

Great. *Would my son hate me once I told him about Devin?*

I heard my text alert and I looked down. Speak of the Devin. He sent a pic of the remains of his dinner on a plate. Then a note.

Love a woman who can cook. Wish you were here with me enjoying this scrumptious meal you prepared. Can't wait to see you at the wedding. Leave your man at home.

Smiling at his text, I started the ignition, praying that somehow the two most important people in my life would forgive me.

8

DEVIN

"Mr. Toussaint, we appreciate your time and willingness to take on this project," the red-haired, stern-faced principal responded.

I smiled. "My firm wants to work with public, private, and charter schools to ensure they have adequate legal protection. With irate parents, school shootings, teachers involved in illegal practices, schools are always susceptible to lawsuits. And your school is the first in our new initiative, so we look forward to our ongoing collaboration. Although the board has already approved our hire, I wanted to meet with you today so you were aware of my personal commitment to this school."

"I am pleased, even more so that you volunteered to do a career day here with our students. Fingers crossed we can get your father to agree to speak that day at school as well."

"I will definitely pull his ear and see if we can make it happen." I chuckled politely, hating that ever since my father had been elected mayor, I became known only as his son and not a successful attorney in my own right. Placing my notepad back in my leather bag, I stood, hand outstretched. "It is never too early for our youth to think about their futures. Anyway, if I can be of help outside of career day, please let my office know."

Grasping my hand warmly, before leading me to the front door of her office, she said, "Ellen must have already gone for the day. I really do need to call one of my parents. Can you find your way back out of the school? If not, give me a few minutes."

"I can figure it out." I waved and headed into the main lobby, excited about my new venture with the schools and about making Royalty my woman soon.

Although I'd been disappointed when I received her text, I loved that she felt comfortable in my home and had taken the time to prepare a delicious dinner for me. Her presence made the house I'd purchased after my divorce a home. I'd never wanted a woman more than I wanted her and would do whatever it took to make her mine. I smiled in anticipation of seeing her at the wedding and taking her home with me, done with waiting for my queen.

I adjusted my bag to open the large double doors once I realized I needed to pull instead of push.

"Hey, let me help you." A young boy with dark brown skin and a headful of curly hair rushed to help me open the door. "You need any help to your car, sir?"

I smiled. "Your parents taught you manners."

The corner of his lips turned down briefly before he responded, "My mama."

"Your mama is doing a good job." I leaned on the door, pulled out my clicker, and tossed it to him, wanting to impress him.

He easily caught it.

"Can you open my trunk from here?"

The boy took a few steps and clicked. His eyes lit up when he saw the lights to my blue Maserati flicker in the parking lot near the walkway. "Dude, is that your car?"

"Yes."

He placed a balled fist over his mouth. "Ooh, that car is bad. I bet it goes fast. What do you do for a living? You must be an entrepreneur or something."

Pleasantly surprised he didn't say athlete or entertainer, I responded, "I'm a lawyer and have my own firm. So yep, I am an entrepreneur."

"My mama's a lawyer, too, but she doesn't have your money."

I bragged, "Tell her she can work for me and soon be driving the same kind of car."

"She should work for you. At least you're black instead of those old stuffy white people."

I quickly looked around, making sure there were no listening ears. "You do know the majority of your school is white?"

He shrugged. "I want to go somewhere else, but my mother says it's the best school in the city."

I acknowledged. "It is. Doesn't mean it's the best for you."

The boy nodded his head enthusiastically. "I try to tell my mama that, but she's not trying to hear it. She's too focused on making sure I have the best of everything. Well...at least the best in her opinion."

"Sorry to tell you, but that's what all good parents want for their children."

I realized we were still standing in the door, and something about this boy appealed to me. Maybe because he reminded me of myself when I was around his age. Underneath his confidence, I sensed vulnerability. I checked my watch. "It's almost four. Shouldn't you be on your way home? What were you about to do?"

"I'm supposed to be in detention. I left to use the restroom."

I raised an eyebrow. "So you were only helping me to avoid going back?"

He shook his head vehemently. "No, sir. You look like you needed help."

"What are you in detention for?"

He said proudly, "My mouth." The boy then spoke in a high-pitched voice and rolled his neck playfully, "Apparently, I don't know when to be quiet and when to speak."

"My mouth got me into trouble a lot, too." I laughed. "Hey, you think you want to talk some more? Maybe I can convince your principal to allow you to spend your detention with me." I came back inside the door.

His eyes brightened and a genuine smile appeared. "Yeah...I mean, yes, sir. What do you want to talk about?"

We started toward the office down the hall. "Whatever you want to talk about."

"Um...I'm not sure." He slowed his steps and I looked down at him, curiously. "You look like you can get a lady or two."

Amused, I responded, "I have had lady friends...so?"

"How do you know if a girl likes you back?"

"You must really like this girl."

He ducked his head. "She's okay."

"What does your mother say?"

"I can't ask her about girls. She thinks I'm too mannish already."

"Your father?"

He studied his Jordans. "Never met him. He doesn't want anything to do with me."

Sensing his sadness, empathizing with him, I said, "I just met you and already I know it's his loss."

The beaming look he gave me was priceless.

We were now standing facing each other in front of the office. "What's your name?"

He put his hand out. "Lil J."

I clasped his hand in mine. "Lil J, call me Mr. D."

9

ROYALTY

"Ladies, we only have an hour before the procession." Mrs. LaSalle rushed over to Raini, still in her robe, as she had her airbrush makeup applied. "How much longer? Raini still has to get dressed."

The makeup artist replied, "Five minutes at the most."

Raini reassured her, "It's okay, Ms. Tiffany. You hired the best wedding planner, who is on her job. We are going to be on time, and the wedding will be the talk of the town."

The petite spitfire straightened the fitted pink skirt of her suit. "Tre is paying top dollar. This wedding better play out without a hitch." She studied Raini's face. "Lighten her eye makeup, it's too sultry for an afternoon wedding."

The exasperated woman replied, "That will add another five minutes."

Mrs. LaSalle retorted, "Did I ask you how long it would take?"

Tresa, Tre's sister and the only bridesmaid, and I tried to hide our laughter. Mrs. LaSalle was something else. She had been a drill sergeant with us, waking us up at practically the crack of dawn to run down the events of the wedding and reception yet again. We were tired from hanging out in the French Quarter for

Raini's bachelorette party. I tried to hide my irritation, partially because I was slightly hungover, but Raini had been smiling all morning and taking everything in stride, including Mrs. LaSalle's bossiness.

Initially Mrs. LaSalle didn't care for Raini, especially after news about Deaux and his previous life in the gang made the news. Over time, Raini and Tre's mother had learned to be cordial to one another, and the wedding had drawn them closer, especially once Tre told her that Raini didn't have a relationship with her mother.

Mrs. LaSalle had softened towards her because her own mother hadn't been involved in her life, either. Today, she had behaved more like a mom than a mother-in-law, especially since Raini's own mother decided not to attend her only child's special day. Mrs. LaSalle had complimented her several times on her hair, which had been blown out and flowed long over her shoulders. Even now she hovered nearby, ensuring that her makeup was perfect, until the wedding planner needed her to head downstairs to get into the car that would take her to St. Louis Cathedral for the wedding.

Meanwhile my stomach had been jittery. I had to use the bathroom twice already and now I had trouble sitting still. "I can't wait until the reception."

"Why are you so nervous when it's my wedding day?" Raini asked as the makeup artist finished the last touches on her already flawless mocha skin.

I retorted, "I'm not nervous."

"Then why are you pacing? You're making *me* nervous," Tresa added.

Raini had bargained with Tre's mother to have a small bridal party in exchange for a huge wedding with over three hundred guests. Tresa and Raini connected easily, and Tresa's unpretentious free spirit and our shared legal profession fit well with me, too. The three of us had had dinner a few times over the past few months and always had a good time. Tre's older brother, TJ, was his best man and Taz, his bodyguard and friend, was his sole groomsman.

"It's just such a big wedding and all of New Orleans will be here." I met Raini's eyes through her reflection in the mirror. "Tell me again why the Toussaints were invited to your wedding?"

Tresa twisted to see her body in the floor-length mirror in the luxurious suite. The pale pink strapless dress complemented her curves, caramel skin and short platinum blonde hair that had been styled into ringlets. "I can answer that, Mere and I may not see eye to eye on most things, but she is a classy lady. She had to extend the invite to the Toussaints or the city would start rumors again about the bad blood between the families. At the end of the day, we're both powerful black families that work best united instead of divided."

Raini added, "And Tresa is only excited because she's feeling Nicholas Toussaint."

"I can see why, he's hot." I bumped Tresa's hip playfully and looked at Raini. "Doesn't she know the Toussaint men are no good?"

Tresa nodded in agreement, then nodded with a knowing smile, "Well...they're good for at least one thing."

I shook my head, unable to hide my smile, knowing firsthand about Devin's sexual prowess. "Definitely. Hope for your sake he's at least better than his cousin."

"Ooh child, no one is as bad as Devin. He will charm the panties off you and throw it in the fire to burn on his way to the next victim."

My stomach knotted at the pretty accurate description of Devin and his reputation with women I'd heard over the years since I'd moved back home. "You've been with him?"

"No. Don't get me wrong, I had a schoolgirl crush on him when he used to be friends with my brothers, but after he stole Nia from Tre...I..." She quickly looked at Raini apologetically. "Please, please say Tre told you about Nia?"

Raini thanked the makeup artist and waited until the door closed behind her to address Tresa. "He did. He told me that was the start of their falling out, and then it changed to hatred when everything went ape-shit crazy during the election."

I pouted. "Well, I didn't know Tre used to date Devin's ex-wife before they were married. Devin went behind Tre's back and started dating her?"

Raini nodded slowly.

Tresa exhaled loudly. "Thank God you already knew why Tre hates Devin or Tre would have killed me. Trust me when I say my brother has never loved any woman but you." Her phone buzzed. "It's Mere. She needs me for a sec. I better run before she comes in here wreaking havoc." She gave me a soft smile. "Hey, I didn't know you were feeling Devin like that. He seems to have calmed down lately, and I don't see him hanging out like he used to do. You two probably need a moment alone after I opened my big mouth. Be right back."

The minute the door to the suite closed, I said, "Why didn't you tell me Devin did that to Tre? No wonder Tre can't stand him. Ever since you and Tre started dating, you've been keeping me out of the loop. For God's sake, you never even told me the whole truth about what happened the day Mr. Deaux died until everything came out in the news. I don't want to lose our closeness, our friendship, because you're marrying the mayor."

She gave me a sharp look through the mirror. "And you never told me the child I helped you raise, my godson's father, is Devin Toussaint, the former *mayor's*, son. We both held secrets, but it doesn't make the love and loyalty we have for each other lessen." She rose from the plush bench she had been sitting on and pulled me down on the nearby sofa next to her. "Royalty, you will never lose me. You were the only person in my life who refused to give up on me when I was too grief-stricken and depressed to be bothered by anyone. I'm sorry I kept so much to myself. It was just easier for me, I guess. Too many years, I blamed myself for my daddy's death and didn't like talking about that horrible day."

Immediately contrite, I touched her hand. "Oh, Rain. I never knew that you blamed yourself. What kind of friend was I that I didn't notice how much you still grieved him?"

"The best friend possible, who reminded me to live again, who pushed me to enjoy my life and encouraged me to give Tre another chance." She nudged my shoulder. "Which is why I didn't tell you about what really happened between Devin and Tre. I don't want to give you any more reasons to avoid him. There's energy between the two of you that even a blind man can see. I've heard the rumors about him and his philandering ways, but if my father can change, maybe he can. Maybe Devin already has. Besides, you need to tell him about Ryder, regardless of what happens between you and him."

I grabbed both of her hands and asked, voice shaking, "I want to tell him...I really do. I have so many conflicting emotions. On one hand, I believe we could make it and be a family, and then I'm frightened that he'll hate me and try to take Ryder away from me because he missed out on so many years. With my family living on the other side of the world, you and Ryder are all I have."

"Why do you keep thinking he's going to do that to you or Ryder? That man seems to really care about you."

"Devin is the biggest alpha male I know, and he may want to get back at me for keeping Ryder away from him all these years. He has the power and resources to do so as one of the most successful litigators in New Orleans, and his dad is the former mayor of New Orleans. Ryder is their only grandchild, only grandson. He might believe he's the better parent to raise a son, and you know Ryder has never been a mama's boy. He would probably choose his father, too."

"That boy loves you and nothing will ever change that. I don't believe Devin would take a son from his mother, even if he's angry with you for not telling him."

"Ask Tre. Devin will do whatever it takes to get something he wants. He may not have known anything about me over the years, but I do know about him. What you heard is not just rumors. He was awful to Tre during the elections, never faithful to his wife, and to know he took her from Tre—someone who was supposed to be his best friend at that time—says a lot about his character."

Raini protested louder, "And my father was a thug who loved the streets, who didn't give a fuck about anyone until he had me. Maybe you and Ryder are what he needs to settle down and be a better man. I know you, and you don't run from anyone."

I admitted ruefully, "Except Devin Toussaint. He could destroy me."

"Or love you until death do you part. You can keep running all you want, but like you just said, he doesn't stop until he gets what he wants. And, best friend, he wants you."

"Why are you so pro Devin? Tre can't stand him, and you don't really know him."

"He's the only one besides you and my family who really knew my daddy and didn't judge him. He wrote me and Tre a few days ago. An old-fashioned letter. He told me how he met my father, and before you ask, he also told me that he wanted to share with you how he knows my father. Devin also asked me to give the letter to Tre because in the letter he apologized to Tre for his transgressions. He didn't think Tre would receive any message from him directly, so he sent it through me."

"What?"

Raini stood and crossed the room to the huge walk-in closet to retrieve a small black envelope. "Lastly, he wanted me to give you this today."

She handed it to me. I traced the gold embossed letters of Devin's monogram before pulling out a gold card with an elegant black font.

Will you do me the honor of saving me a dance?

I held the unexpectedly, unbelievably sweet and thoughtful

gesture to my heart and looked at Raini. "You think Devin and me are inevitable?"

"As parents of Ryder, yes. As for your love story, I certainly hope so."

Someone knocked on the door. Probably the wedding coordinator. It was time for my best friend to marry the love of her life. The only man with whom she had been intimate. The man she fell in love with when they shared a kiss so many years ago at a high school dance and shortly after never saw each other again until last year.

"Enough about me. Today is your special day." I squealed, "I can't believe you're getting married to Tre LaSalle. Crazy how just a year ago today he walked into your bookstore."

She blinked back tears. "I miss my daddy so much today. I used to say I didn't want a wedding since I didn't have my daddy to give me away. Tre made me believe that I can walk alone, head held high and celebrate our love. He made dreams I didn't even know I had come true. I keep thinking that sooner or later, I'm going to wake from this amazing fairytale. I wouldn't know what to do without him or Tracie. They're my family now."

I tapped her shoulder with mine. "Just don't forget about me and Ryder."

"Never, especially that big head boy who is going to be another Devin with the way he already likes the girls."

"Lord, I hope not. One Devin Toussaint in this world is enough."

※

OUR EYES MET THE MOMENT I GLIDED DOWN THE WHITE ROSE petals and tea-lighted aisle on the arms of TJ, Tre's older brother. Sitting at the end of the second row reserved for his family and other New Orleans elite, Devin's teary-eyed gaze did not waver from me as if I was his bride.

I reluctantly dragged my focus from him to see a handsome,

rather stoic Tre. He waited at the end, hands behind his back, facial expression stern, so unlike the smiling, laughing Tre to whom I'd become accustomed. When TJ and I made it to the altar, I winked and whispered, "She is so ready to marry you."

Instantly, his face relaxed and his lips curved at my words, and at the evidence of his love for Raini, I mentally blessed the makeup artist for this waterproof eye makeup. Once I found my position, I looked down the aisle and witnessed Tracie, Tre's beautiful nine-year old daughter, appearing almost ethereal in her long white dress as she dropped white and pink rose petals on her way to the altar.

When she drew closer to Tre, she said proudly, "Hey, Daddy. You look good."

"Hey, sweetie, you look amazing, too." He waved and the guests *ahhed* at their obvious affection toward one another.

Then suddenly the soft romantic jazz music changed to Mr. Deaux's favorite song, Luther Vandross's "Here and Now" and everyone rose to their feet. Raini Blue Thibodeaux, my best friend, never looked more beautiful, confident, happy, serene, and in love, wearing a dress she designed.

Her wedding gown was made of a pink so pale it almost appeared white. With a strapless bodice made of real white roses that cinched at her small waist and a full sparkly tulle bottom, it belonged on the latest fashion runway. Raini proceeded down the aisle alone in honor of her father, smiling at various love ones, her white lace train flowing behind her. At the sight of her handsome groom waiting expectantly at the altar with a wide, trembling smile, tears unchecked flowed down her face. I met Devin's gaze again, the only person not watching Raini, and I prayed for true love and that he and I were possible.

THE RECEPTION WAS HELD IN THE NOPSI HOTEL, OWNED BY Sheila Johnson, the former wife of Bob Johnson, the first black billionaire. In the divorce proceedings, she had been awarded half of his three billion dollars. She used some of her money and redeveloped an old electric company building into a world class, four-star hotel, replete with the traditional brick walls of older hotels in the historic downtown and French Quarter area, a rooftop bar, and pool area.

TJ and I headed into the bridal party suite to take more photos. We could hear the music blasting and the lively chatter of guests arriving at the reception hall. Raini pulled me away from TJ to help her change dresses in the private bathroom before she went to take more photos in one of the rooms in the suite. She left the bathroom, and I stayed longer, trying to gather my thoughts. This felt like high school all over again, when all I could think about was seeing my crush. My stomach ached in anticipation of seeing him at the reception, and I wondered if he would approach me or if he expected me to come to him. More importantly, I longed to know how a relationship with him would be this time.

I didn't know if Devin had arrived yet. Once the horses and carriages brought the wedding party to the hotel, we had been led away from the reception hall. While looking at my reflection, fluffing my wavy hair to hang down over my breasts, highlighting the spattering of glitter on my cleavage, the door behind me opened. I locked eyes with Devin through the mirror.

Breathlessly, I said, "Hey."

"Hey." He strolled over and stood behind me, watching me, watching us in the mirror, before he curved his hands to my waist. The span of his large hands from the sides of my breasts to my hips made my waist seem tiny in comparison. "I wanted a quiet moment alone with you."

My voice trembled. "It's about to get crazy."

"Yes...it is." Devin moved my hair gently to my right side, before he placed his hand back on my waist. His index fingers traced my now hardened nipples through my dress as he said, "I'm not an emotional man, but watching you walk down that aisle, so fucking beautiful, so hot, so amazing, you brought tears to my eyes. All those men wondering who you were and if they have a chance with you and they don't."

I asked quietly, mesmerized by his hypnotic caress. "Why?"

He placed his full lips on my neck and sucked my skin. My clit throbbed almost painfully at the pressure of his mouth on my neck, his insistent fingers against my erect buds. I rubbed the top of his bent head, my fingers enjoying the feel of his soft wavy hair, pushing my ass on his erect dick, encouraging his selfish, possessive marking of me. He deepened his attack on my neck while grinding on me, a reminder that he knew how to stroke the hell out of my pussy. I wanted desperately to bend over and let him fuck me.

Then someone knocked on the door.

Devin lifted his head, lightly panting, his claim already on my skin. He looked down at his groin and adjusted his tailored pants to mask the evidence of his desire. I held on to the counter, still using the mirror to observe him, trying to calm my beating heart, my flushed face, and my aching sex. Without another word, he unlocked the door and greeted a surprised Tresa before walking away.

Tresa sauntered into the bathroom with a knowing smile and I practically wilted, needing his presence like flowers need light. "What just happened here?"

Touching my neck, I turned to look at her, my fate forever sealed. "Devin Toussaint."

10

DEVIN

Marking her may have been selfish and childish, but she needed to know that she was mine and mine alone. Walking away from Royalty had to be one of the hardest things I have ever done. Had Tresa not knocked when she did, I would've been inside her, reception be damned.

A part of me wanted to snatch her up and never let go until she accepted that we were meant to be. The better part of me knew that she battled with herself over loving me, and I needed her to come to me willingly. Maybe Nicholas had been right, and she found out I was married during the time of our involvement. That would more than explain her reluctance to be with me. I had to re-gain her trust.

Heading into the grand ballroom, my sexual energy shifted to dread. Ever since my separation from Nia, I hated these events where I had to be on display for the city of New Orleans. Women jockeying for my attention, people watching to see if there would be any drama between the black elite, especially between the Toussaint and the LaSalle families.

I had to remind myself that I only attended for the beautiful, willful woman intent on wreaking havoc with my heart, and for my mother. When my mother called all excited because she'd received an invitation to Tre's wedding, and that it included an open invite to the Toussaint family, I reluctantly agreed to attend. She'd been the one most hurt in the feud between the families—a feud I started when I chose potential love over friendship.

Mama and Tre's mother, Tiffany LaSalle, had become close friends through their husbands' friendship. Unlike Mrs. LaSalle, the now retired educator, my mother had been a homemaker dedicated to her husband and only son. Mrs. LaSalle and I used to beg her to go back to college and finish her teaching degree. She would have been an excellent teacher with her pleasant demeanor and kind guidance.

I wanted her to have an identity outside of being my mother and Mrs. Derrick Toussaint, but she would always claim she belonged to too many volunteer and charity organizations to commit to school. I believed if she had a career or profession she loved, she would have left my father years ago. I often wondered if Mrs. LaSalle, who probably knew intimate details of my father's transgressions with other women, thought so, too.

My mother waved to me as soon as I stepped into the lavishly decorated hall. Always classy, Mrs. LaSalle had placed our family table in the front next to their tables. Ma remained a stunning creole woman with her naturally long brown hair pinned up in a bun and her pale blue evening dress fitting her well-maintained body. She could easily pass for someone a decade or more younger than her sixty-two years, and she'd worked hard to maintain her looks, always afraid of losing my father to one of his women.

She stood when I approached the table, arms open and welcoming. I hugged her to me, inhaling her familiar scent. "I was hoping you would make it to the reception. When you left the wedding in such a hurry, I didn't think you would be here."

I'd chosen to sit away from my parents at the wedding and rushed off as soon as the wedding ended, hoping to catch Royalty before the reception started.

I winked. "This is the best part, Ma. All the free food and drinks."

"Why did you rush off?" asked my father, who had walked in from the other side of the table. My father, tall, dark-skinned, bald, with a graying mustache and beard, had already taken off his jacket and loosened his tie. "I thought maybe you were afraid to be around this much success."

"No, that would be you since you lost to Tre in the election." My father liked to take digs at my decision to focus on being an attorney rather than join the political fray once he became mayor.

"He won't win a second term."

"I hope he does," I retorted.

"Not here," Ma warned.

Someone clasped my shoulder. "Hey, fam."

Instantly calming at the sound of Nicholas's voice, I turned around and dapped him, pulling him in for a hug, our clasped hands in between our bodies. "I didn't see you at the wedding."

"I was late, so I sat in the back."

I shook my head at my cousin's poor concept of time. "Man, you can't get anywhere on time to save your life."

"Look, I'm here now and that's all that matters."

"Glad you're here."

He moved around me to smack my mother's cheek. "Auntie Chris, don't you look good. You trying to get some numbers tonight?"

"Oh, boy, stop it." She blushed at his compliment.

"Hey, Unc." Nicholas and my father embraced. I used to be envious of their affable relationship, which my father never fostered with me. I'd long ago accepted that my father and I would never be close. As much as I hated to admit it, he and I were alike, despite my best intentions to be different than him. We were both arrogant, stubborn, and hated being wrong, which meant our disagreements were rarely resolved.

"Is your mother coming to the reception?" Ma asked Nicholas.

He shrugged. "Your guess is as good as mine."

My father frowned. "You haven't spoken to her?"

"No," he responded, not quite curtly. "I don't keep tabs on a grown woman."

"Let me call her." My father pulled out his cell, his concern for his wayward younger sister ever present. He'd even taken Nicholas in to raise at thirteen years old because my aunt, a single mother, didn't have the patience to be a parent. And his father rarely bothered to acknowledge his existence. Maybe that's why I didn't begrudge my cousin for having a closer relationship with my father than I did.

"You do that and tell me how that goes." Nicholas seemed annoyed before plastering a smile on his face to keep up appearances. "Come on, Dev, I need a drink."

***

WE STEPPED UP TO ONE OF SEVERAL OPEN BARS. NICHOLAS asked, "Your usual?"

I nodded.

He ordered, "Give me a whiskey sour and a Ketel One and tonic."

"You good?"

"I'm good." Nicholas tapped the bar. "Tre is finally off the market, breaking half these women's hearts. Surprised he hadn't married sooner, especially when he decided to run for mayor as a never-been-married single dad. We thought that would hurt him in the election."

I shrugged. "Too many non-traditional families to think that matters anymore. I was there when he proposed, and I don't think he would have ever married if he hadn't seen Raini again."

"That's some love out of a romance movie. I've never felt that way about any woman, or at least I don't think so."

I responded, "You would know."

"Speaking of romance movies, I saw your girl Royalty strutting down that aisle like a model." He whistled. "Cuz, I understand why you couldn't get over her. She's definitely sexy wifey material."

I smiled. "She is. Tonight is the night."

"Did she bring her man?" Nicholas picked up his drink.

"Told her not to and even if she did, it doesn't matter."

Nicholas grinned and dapped me off. "That's the Dev I know."

Holding our respective drinks, we both turned to face the party, observing the smiles, laughter, and dancing guests. A couple of beautiful women smiled at us. Nicholas grinned wide. "I'm taking someone home tonight myself. Too many beautiful women in one place, feeling all romantic. What you think about Tresa? She looked damn good walking down that aisle, rocking that short hair."

I swallowed my drink. "Tre's little sister? I don't think of her in that way."

"Dev, you know when a woman is fine no matter who her people are."

"Of course, she's pretty, but she like my fam, even if we don't talk anymore. You trying to get with her?"

"We hung out and flirted at the Zulu Ball last month. I've always thought she was sexy, but something is different about her."

"You know I'm the last to judge you, but we already have bad blood with the LaSalles. Last thing we need is for one of us to hurt one of them again."

"Tresa just like me, she's not trying to be serious. Just have fun. Neither one of us trying to settle down any time soon."

I smiled. "True. She does like to party."

Nicholas's chuckle abruptly stopped. "Trouble at six o'clock."

I looked straight ahead and saw the woman who always thought she should have been Mrs. Toussaint, Melanie Andrews.

She had always been a striking woman with her raven-colored hair, light brown eyes, honey tanned skin, and killer legs which she always took the opportunity to display. Tonight was no exception. Her red sparkly dress had a high split, and her stance demanded attention to her shapely thighs and calves.

"One of the reasons I dreaded tonight. Running into my past," I muttered.

"Cuz, I already see several of your pasts."

"Yeah, but she's the most bitter." I sipped on my drink, watching her saunter my way. I'd really fucked up when I started up with her again during my marriage and right after my divorce.

Nicholas greeted Mel with a chaste kiss on the cheek and a polite hug before walking away, shaking his head.

I smiled, trying to keep the vibe pleasant. Two years ago, she had flattened my tires and tried to scratch the shit out of my face when I told her that we were done and I had no intentions of marrying her or any woman. "Beautiful as always, Mel."

"Thank you. I chose this dress with you in mind." She moved closer to me. "No hug for an old girlfriend?"

Refusing to acknowledge that she'd dressed for me, I used one arm to embrace her briefly. "I didn't expect to see you here. How did you get an invite?"

"Oh, I'm not good enough to be invited?"

I clenched my jaw. She always thought I'd chosen Nia as my wife because she came from money and Mel didn't, which couldn't have been further from the truth. "You know I didn't mean it like that. This is a private affair, and you don't know the LaSalles or the bride's family."

She said smugly. "My boyfriend works in Tre's office. He's over at the table reserved for the staff."

"I'm happy for you." I downed the rest of my drink. "You better go back before he gets jealous."

"Does he have a reason to be jealous?"

I replied honestly, "No. I just don't want any trouble. I have no idea what you may have told him about me, and if he sees you smiling in my face, body leaned toward me, then he's going to have a problem. And I really have more important things to do than to get in a fight over an ex who I no longer want."

She hissed, "Why do you have to be such an asshole?"

"Speaking truth, Mel. Now go on back to your boyfriend before you make a scene."

Mel placed one hand on her hip. "Ooh, wouldn't want to tarnish your precious image."

"It's obvious you're not going to leave me the fuck alone, so I'll walk away." I slammed my empty glass on a nearby table, turned and headed toward the entrance, needing some air. Seeing her was a reminder of the man I used to be, a man who had hurt women because I could.

As I approached the door, security blocked it off to announce the entrance of the bridal party and the bride and groom. Seeing Royalty on the arm of TJ bothered the fuck out of me. He'd whispered something in her ear, and she smiled as they strode into the room with her arm tucked under his. I couldn't help but think they made an attractive couple, and TJ was one of the good guys. He definitely didn't have the baggage I had.

I couldn't blame Royalty if she chose someone like him over me. Suddenly, everyone cheered when Tre and Raini entered. Raini had changed into a pale pink halter dress that skimmed her curves and removed her hair from the bun, her hair in loose waves over her shoulders. She was indeed stunning, and Tre was a lucky man. My envy unchecked, I watched a glowing Raini and Tre on the happiest day of their lives, wishing this day had been mine and Royalty's.

I had second thoughts about staying for the reception, thinking maybe I didn't deserve Royalty, until I noticed that she had brushed her hair behind her shoulders, my passion mark visible for all eyes to see. I watched as she seemingly unconsciously touched her neck as the bridal party were seated in the front of the hall. Knowing that she hadn't tried to hide the red flush on her neck boosted my confidence, which had dwindled since I spoke to my father and had my run-in with Mel. I wouldn't be me if I gave up on her now.

I straightened my shoulders and began to move about the party, speaking to various friends, acquaintances, political foes, all while observing the bridal party mingling and eating. I wondered if Raini had given Royalty my card and when I would get another moment with Royalty.

An hour into the reception, I noticed Royalty at the bar alone, amazingly. I sidled up to her and placed my arm around her perfect waist. "Ms. James."

She smiled flirtatiously. "Mr. Toussaint."

Damn. Just her voice made me hard. "Do you have a minute?"

Royalty leaned into me. "No, but I had to sneak away to see you."

"At the bar? Our tables are nearer to each other than this bar. Why didn't you just come to me?"

She winked. "So much more fun for you to come to me."

I took her drink out of her hand and pulled her behind me.

Royalty protested, "Hey, I needed that drink. They only giving us champagne at the tables. Where are we going?"

Uncaring that tongues would start wagging, I walked through the reception holding her hand. "I want you to meet someone."

We walked back to my table and my mother smiled as we approached. "Is this the Royalty I've heard so much about?" I'd recently confided in my mother about my feelings for Royalty, something I hadn't done since I was a teenager when I would share my crushes with her.

"Yes, this is she. Royalty, this is my mother, Crystal Toussaint."

My mother complimented, "Devin, she's beautiful, isn't she?"

I squeezed Royalty's hand, beaming with pride. "Yes, she's gorgeous."

Raising a curious brow at me, Royalty bent to hug my

mother. "A pleasure to meet you, and I see where your son gets his handsome looks."

When Royalty straightened, my mother responded, "Everyone thinks he looks like his father because of their skin color, but my boy looks just like me."

"Where's Dad?" I asked, searching the room.

The light dimmed in her eyes. "Oh, you know your father has to always socialize, meet the people."

"Yeah." I hated that my father's tendency to stray made it difficult for my mother to genuinely enjoy events like this. She never knew if an old or new flame lurked in the crowd. "Do you want me to find him?"

"No, no." She waved away the suggestion.

"I can sit with you."

"Don't mind me, I'm enjoying seeing some of my old friends. Me and Tiffany have even made lunch plans, hoping this wedding bridges the gap between the families again." She touched Royalty's arm. "You're the bride's best friend, right?"

"Yes."

"Maybe with you being Devin's lady, he and Tre can finally become friends again."

"Oh...Mrs. Toussaint, I'm not..."

I half jerked Royalty behind me, not wanting her to tell my mother that we weren't together. "Ma, let's not bring up old stuff. Tre and Raini invited us to the wedding, and that's enough for now." I kissed her cheek. "She still has maid of honor duties, but I just wanted to introduce my two favorite women to each other."

"Okay, dear." She touched Royalty's hand. "We will have to meet for brunch or something at the house."

"I would love that, Mrs. Toussaint."

The minute we were out of earshot, she looked up at me. "Your mother is sweet. I see where you get your good looks."

"I can tell she already likes you."

She squeezed my hand. "Why did you tell your mother we're together?"

I gazed down into her amused beautiful face. "Because we are."

Someone cleared his throat, and TJ stood before us with an amused smile. We shook hands rather formally for the friends we used to be. "Your mother really went all out for this one." I'd been one of his groomsmen in his small intimate wedding years ago.

He quirked his thick brows. "It's for her precious son."

I nodded, fully aware of their mother's favoritism towards Tre. TJ and I had been close before Tre and me since we'd attended the same high school. I missed his friendship, too. He'd always been the level-headed one out of all of us, eschewing our wild partying ways and politics for life as a business executive for a start-up in the suburbs with his wife. TJ had been divorced longer than me, and because we were no longer friends, I hadn't been privy to why what appeared to be a fairytale romance had ended.

TJ addressed Royalty. "Raini is looking for you. We still need to take a couple more photos." He placed a hand on her lower back and she shot an apologetic look over one shoulder as he took her away from me.

11

ROYALTY

"I didn't realize you and Devin were a thing?"

In the private suite, TJ and I waited in comfortable Victorian chairs for our turn to take photos again. Raini and Tre were taking pics with Tresa and Taz in the next room.

"He's an old friend."

He smiled at me. "I would tell you to be careful and ask you out, but it's way too clear that you're gone over him." TJ and I had gotten to know one another during the pre-wedding festivities and had engaged in harmless flirting. As handsome as he was with his curly dark hair, twin dimples, and café au lait skin, he didn't have anything on the swag and natural charisma of Devin.

I protested, "It's not that clear."

"I was your escort down the aisle and peeped how you almost stumbled when you saw him, and he didn't help, staring at you all mesmerized at the end of the row."

"You were paying that much attention to me?" I teased. "You saying you like me?"

"I'm saying I'm a single man who knows a good woman when he sees one. I'm also too old to go after a woman who's into someone else, especially if she has questionable taste in men."

I playfully tapped his firm bicep. "Questionable taste?"

"I call it like I see it." He shrugged.

I didn't bother to protest the truth of my interest in Devin. I needed answers. "You used to be his friend too, right? Is he that bad with women?"

"You got me breaking the bro code, which I still try to honor, even to my former friends."

I coaxed, "Come on, we're practically family now."

He groaned. "Fine, but you can't tell Devin I said anything." He draped an arm around my neck. "He and I were friends first because we attended the same high school, but he and Tre had more in common and became best friends when we were adults. Between you and me, I don't really have anything against Devin. I didn't think it was a big deal that Devin and Nia started dating because my brother was seeing other women at that time. A fact that Devin knew as well. More than anything, Tre's ego was hurt that Nia chose Devin. I tried to get him to forgive Devin, but he wouldn't.

"I'm the only member of the family that could care less about politics, and I only sided with Tre during the election out of loyalty to my family. But to answer your question, he is a decent dude who loves his family and fights for the underdog. Unfortunately, he is also a lot like his father, who doesn't know the meaning of monogamy. Granted, we haven't hung out as friends for a long time so he may have changed. The divorce may have humbled him because he definitely never pictured Nia leaving him, especially after Nya was born."

I mused about Devin's ex. "He must have really loved her." Grimacing, I stretched my aching feet.

TJ shrugged. "That's something you have to ask him. In my humble opinion, he got married because he felt like it was time, and she made a suitable wife. That's just my opinion. Because when you marry for love, you don't keep cheating on your spouse." He suddenly removed his arm to bend and pull off my heels and placed them next to my feet. "There."

I breathed a sigh of relief. "I hope I can put them back on when I need to."

TJ resumed his position and lifted his arm. "You can rest against me."

"Are you flirting with me?" I laid my head on the side of his firm chest and looked up into his handsome face.

He dimpled. "Do you love Devin?"

I popped up. "How could you even tell that? Maybe I'm just attracted to him."

TJ laughed loudly. "You answered my question, and I am most definitely *not* flirting with you. A waste of my time and yours."

"One more question."

He rolled his eyes. "What? Seriously, go ask your new boo."

It was my turn to laugh. "You are cool people, you know that?"

"I've heard that a time or two. What's your question?"

"Why are you still single? I can tell you're not the player type, probably never been."

"You mean as bad as Tre and Devin? Because I've had my share of women."

"Now whose ego is talking? Not that you can't have more than one woman, but you seem like the monogamous type. I know we've only had a few conversations since the engagement, but you're a certifiable catch. So, what's the deal?"

He grew pensive and looked down at the floor before he met my gaze again. "Married the right woman at the wrong time, and I haven't found the right woman at the right time yet."

A waitress carrying champagne walked past us at that moment. I grabbed two flutes and gave him one. I lifted my flute in the air. "May we both find that right person at the right time."

Tapping his glass with mine, TJ agreed. "Amen."

THE OBJECT OF MY MOST EROTIC THOUGHTS SPENT THE FESTIVE evening working the reception with his charming cousin, chatting with his parents and other dignitaries of the city, including his former father-in-law, Congressman Saint and his wife, Shelly. Meanwhile, I danced with abandon with the bride and groom, their families, and other wedding guests.

Before I could ask him to dance with me, the band played a softer tune and Tre announced through a microphone, "If I can have your attention, my wife has decided that we shouldn't toss our bouquet and garter. She wants us to appoint..." Raini whispered in his ear. "Sorry, used to being the mayor. She wants us to give it to two people of our choice. We choose...Royalty James and Devin Toussaint."

I shot a surprised look at Raini, who had already walked toward an equally stunned Devin. He recovered quicker than I did and smiled as she put her arm under his and escorted him to the front of the room, where staff had surreptitiously placed a white rose decorated plush chair.

Tre presented Raini's pink and white rose bouquet before taking my hand and whispering in my ear, "This is not my idea. You can still back out."

I smiled. "I'm good."

"Alright, don't say I didn't warn you."

I gave him a big familial smooch on his cheek. "Thank you. Nice to know I have another big brother looking out for me."

He nudged my shoulder. "Team Royalty."

"Team Tre."

He escorted me to the chair where Devin waited with a mischievous grin, waving the garter in his hand. Tre and Devin acknowledged each other with a nod before Tre joined his new bride at the edge of the semi-circle of guests that now surrounded us. Once I settled in my chair, holding the bouquet, I looked up at Devin and with a pleasant smile warned, "Don't try anything in front of all these people."

He only winked before he kneeled and lifted my silver

Louboutin and placed the lace fabric over my heel. He then caressed my leg, placing delicious kisses on my heated skin as he inched the garter higher. I gripped the flowers, willing myself not to close my eyes in pleasure as the audience cheered and clapped loudly at his lascivious behavior.

Once his hands disappeared under my dress, and he met my gaze, his expression no longer taunting or playful, I prayed that I wouldn't orgasm in front of all these people. He pushed the garter higher, almost near the apex of my thighs, my panties now soaked with need for him. He kept one hand on my leg, and moved the bouquet in my hands to the floor before he quietly demanded, "Kiss me."

Without breaking our shared gaze, I pulled his chin closer until my lips almost touched his, and shook my head. "No."

The guests went wild at my response and wilder when he rose, lifting me to my feet before dipping me over one arm and capturing my lips in a breath-taking kiss in front of everyone. I wrapped my arms around his strong neck to maintain my balance. His kiss left me feeble-minded and dizzy with excitement. When he finally straightened, he kept his arms around me, an adoring smile on his face. I didn't even care that he'd made his intentions toward me public and that we were going to be the center of gossip at the mayor's wedding. All I wanted was to be in his arms the rest of the night.

Caressing the waves at the back of his well-groomed head, I asked, "Ready for that dance you requested?"

His lips curved into the widest smile. "I wasn't sure if Raini gave you the message."

"She did." I smoothed the wrinkles in his forehead at his unspoken question as I said, "I was waiting for the right moment."

Oblivious to the gawking audience, we started swaying to the music in our hearts before the band began playing again. Gradually, guests flooded the space around us, the party back in full swing. Within his warm embrace, I melded my softness into his hard body. I didn't want to fight our powerful attraction any longer. My ear rested against his chest, and I could feel the rhythmic beats of his heart. "Devin?"

"Hmm," he murmured, his eyes closed.

"Take me home."

His eyes remained closed though he placed a lingering kiss on my temple. "I have a condo within walking distance."

I tapped the back of head. "What if I brought a date?"

Devin looked down at me. "I told you not to. Glad you listened. Wouldn't want to embarrass him since you were going to be mine tonight." He kissed the tip of my nose.

I grinned. "You really are persistent until you get what you want."

Devin's deep chuckle traveled straight to my core. "Always."

Tracing the contours of his face, I said, "Mr. Toussaint, you really are too much."

His desire for me emanated potently from his soul, and he didn't say another word as he took my hand and pulled me toward him, toward love.

12

ROYALTY

Only a short walk from the hotel, time seemed to drag the closer we approached Devin's building. I shivered when the cold air of the lobby hit my bare skin, and he rubbed my arms, trying to warm me. Once in the elevator, he propped himself against the back and pulled me into his arms.

We were silent riders as others got on and off, the sexual tension building with every floor that we passed as I leaned against him, his stiff erection in my lower back. I held tightly to his hand as we walked to the door of his condo. Wordlessly, he led me past the open living area, the huge inviting bed in the dark bedroom, and we went into the steamy bathroom lit only by candles. Red rose petals littered the floor and around the tub. Bubbles almost overflowed from the huge sunken tub.

"Thought you might appreciate a soak after a long day."

I looked at Devin in astonishment, overcome with all the conflicting emotions I'd had for him over the years and the romanticism of this moment that he'd somehow planned while we partied the night away. "This is so beautiful. I can't believe you did all this."

Devin gently brushed my lips with his. "You deserve this and so much more."

"You've just been so sweet with all your thoughtful gifts." Needing to be closer to him, I pushed his suit jacket off his muscled shoulders and wrapped my arms around his neck, pressing my softness into his firmness. Gazing into his dark and sexy eyes, I admitted, "I have never craved a man as much as you. I think of you even when I'm not trying."

"Well, there's not a day that goes by when I'm not obsessed with thoughts of you, wondering when you'll give me another chance."

"You've always made me throw caution to the wind, and tonight is no different. I want to feel you deep inside of me, no barriers between us. Just your dick inside my pussy." I punctuated my words with a slow lick of his lips.

He inhaled sharply before he ravished my mouth. The scruff of his beard and mustache grazed my face as our tongues mated ardently. After delicious seconds passed, he lifted his head, removing my arms from around his neck, his voice dripping with sex, and demanded, "Take it off."

Ready and willing to do anything he asked of me, I bit the corner of my lips and reached behind me to unzip enough to lower my straps. Revealing my breasts, I felt powerful yet vulnerable as he watched me. I licked both my thumbs and rubbed first my right my nipple and then my left.

Devin's chest rose and fell rapidly, and he couldn't tear his eyes from my chocolate orbs that glistened in the candlelight. I then slid the rest of the dress over my hips until it pooled around my heels. The tip of his index finger leisurely traced the deep V in between my breasts, slowly traveling down to my stomach, my belly button, the top edge of my lace black panties.

Without warning, he ripped the fabric off me, and I gasped. Standing before him naked—pussy wet, nipples rigid—I ached for his touch.

He lowered his head and licked my right nipple before pulling the stiff bud in his mouth. I grabbed his head to my breast, urging him to never stop. His hand moved down over my abs to cup my mound as one long finger slipped inside my folds to rub my clit.

I hissed, "Fuck. It's been too long, I don't want to wait any longer."

Devin then placed his finger inside of me as he stared into my eyes, his eyes hooded. "It has been a long time, and I have my doubts you can handle me now."

He started sliding his finger in and out, and I held on to his arms, to maintain my balance. "Ooh, baby...I can handle whatever you give me."

Devin chuckled softly. "Take your heels off."

I complied, using my toes to press down on my heels to step out of my pumps while he continued to finger me. Our past sexual escapades were always hot and fast, the intense heat between us not allowing for a slow burn. Tonight, Devin seemed intent on taking his time as he assisted me in the warm, soothing, heavenly tub. I slid down against the fiberglass until my naked body had been covered by the white puffs of fragrant soap, and I looked up at him, anticipating his next move.

With a pleased smile at my obvious satisfaction with the drawn bath, he began to unbutton his shirt until it too flowed to the floor. In the dim light, his beautiful, mahogany, naturally toned, chest, abs, and sinewy arms seemed more luminous. He unbuttoned his expertly tailored pants and stepped out of his own Louboutin shoes for men. I couldn't drag my eyes away as he finally lowered his boxer briefs and revealed his thick, long, and hard member. I remembered well all the rapturous things his body used to do to mine.

Devin stepped into the large tub meant for two and laid his naked chest on top of mine. The steam, the candles, the flowers, the warm water swirling around us, enhanced the eroticism of our skin to skin contact. Tongue dipping in and out of my mouth, he moved my arms above my head and placed my legs on either side of the tub. Licking down my gyrating body, savoring each of my areolas without touching my nipples was positively maddening. He went underwater and soon he indulged on my already swollen button, while his hands massaged my breasts. I whimpered at the bold caress of his tongue lavishing the most erogenous part of me. I rubbed the back of his wavy head, relaxed my legs, luxuriating in the act of oral sex.

When I started to undulate faster against his mouth, he held his breath long enough to lick me until I reached the brink of a mind-blowing orgasm. Devin raised his head, delaying my much-needed sexual gratification, looking even hotter with water dripping down his face. His lips curved into a sexy grin as he moved back up my body to kiss me, evidence of his journey down below on his mouth. He then grabbed a handful of my hair and pulled my head back as he poised his thick staff at the entrance to my sex, and whispered, "Tell me you love me."

I only smiled.

He jerked my head back and rained kisses up my exposed neck while his erect tip continued to tease me. "Tell me."

"And if I don't, you're going to punish me and not fuck me?"

He nodded, kissing me deeply, circling his ass just enough to make me mewl. "You've always loved my dick... I need you to love all of me."

I whispered against his lips, "You don't play fair."

"Not when it comes to something I want." Devin pushed himself almost inside of me.

"Damn...you feel so good. What if I'm only telling you what you want to hear to get what I want?" I widened my legs and gyrated against him, and he closed his eyes tight. Impressed with his restraint, the need for him to penetrate so urgent, so strong, I added, "Why torture the both of us? I could say I love you just to have your body again."

He opened his eyes. "You don't say things you don't mean."

"And I don't say things until I'm ready. It's too soon to say we love each other."

"Not for me."

"Oh, so you love me?" I stared into his dark brown eyes, daring him to say it first.

"Yes...with all my heart," Devin admitted quietly before he entered me smoothly and deeply.

I closed my legs around his waist, and we exhaled together as our bodies melded into one. His strokes were deliberate, sensual, measured, and designed to make my toes curl. The rhythm of his tongue in my mouth matched his languid hip action. My hands slid down his back to his taut ass, pressing him even deeper inside of me, relishing his thickness that now filled my core. His wet chest moved up and down my breasts, teasing my aching nipples. I couldn't get enough of him, didn't know if I would ever again be completely sexually satiated if he stopped wanting me.

I moaned expletives in his mouth as he increased his rhythm, starting the spiral of rapturous sensations all over again. Placing my legs on his shoulders and entwining our fingers, Devin began to thrust relentlessly until my legs, my thighs, my pussy quivered in reaction. His breathing suddenly became more erratic, matching my panting, his guttural moans loud as my voice calling his name, and all too soon we reached the precipice of our passion, and I exploded all around him while he poured himself deep within me.

※

LATER THAT NIGHT IN HIS BED, AS I CRADLED HIS HEAD against my chest while he slept, instead of basking in the beautiful rays of hopeful love, all I could feel were the clouds of fear that somehow I wouldn't get my fairytale ending.

13
DEVIN

Slowly waking up, expecting Royalty's warm, supple body beside mine, I reached for her and touched a cool, empty space. I sat up, frantically searching for her, her clothes, anything that would let me know she didn't leave me. The idea of being without her ever again had become painful and incomprehensible. She was mine now, and I would do anything to keep her.

She spoke quietly in the morning light. "I'm over here."

With relief, my eyes rested on Royalty, staring out the window, beautiful even with slightly swollen eyes, her uncombed, messy hair, and wearing my shirt.

I tapped the area next to me. "It's early, come back to bed."

Royalty shook her head. "I have too much on my mind."

Afraid of her answer yet needing to know, I asked, "What are you thinking about?"

Turning to face me, her voice remained soft, reflective. "Last night was magical and intense, but in the light of day, I wonder whether you and I are right. You're a complicated man, Devin. People talk, and your life is full of secrets and lies, and over the years, you've left a trail of broken hearts behind you."

I protested, "Says the even more complicated woman, who

can't seem to make up her mind about me and who I know little about."

She crossed her arms over her chest. "My heart is at stake, and I don't give it freely."

"Yet you trusted me enough with your body to not use protection."

Royalty retorted, "And I told you that I throw caution to the wind when it comes to you...but you can so destroy me, Devin."

Hitting the mattress hard, I declared, "I'm not that man anymore."

She gave a short laugh. "How many women last night at the reception had you been with?"

There were at least six besides Mel, but I didn't want to make this situation worse, so I pleaded, "Last night I claimed you openly, making it clear to anyone who cared that you're mine."

"Without asking me, Devin."

"You didn't seem to mind at the reception, nor when I branded your body with my name all night."

Royalty glared at me. "Being fucking amazing in bed doesn't mean you should be my man."

I tugged on my beard, trying to understand her resistance after such an incredible night of shared passion. "I expected to wake up to love, instead you're way over there, practically snapping my head off. Why are you fighting me so hard? We have something undeniable."

"I didn't care if you had someone when I met you. I'm older and wiser and can't be that woman who turns a blind eye to your indiscretions."

I moved to the edge of the bed, anxious about where this conversation was headed. "My indiscretions? I won't apologize for my past behavior with other women to you. I was a bastard to the women in my life, and I've apologized to the ones I hurt the most. No, you have a chip on your shoulder about whatever happened between us in the past. Either we can start anew, or we don't, but I can't fix whatever issues you have with how you and I ended unless you tell me why you ghosted me. I didn't break your heart or mistreat you. In fact, I wanted to keep seeing you."

Her beautiful face suddenly contorted into anger and hurt as she accused, "Because you were fucking married, Devin!"

I kept my voice even, hoping to soothe her, relieved I finally understood the reason for her trepidation. "How did you know that I was married at the time we met?"

"At least you didn't try to lie," she snorted derisively.

"I don't have time for lies anymore. How did you find out?"

She stared at me like I'd asked the stupidest question ever. "I'm from New Orleans, remember?"

I shrugged. "And? We met and dated in D.C. At the time you had visions of working in legislation on The Hill and had no intention of returning to New Orleans."

"I saw your wedding announcement in the paper in the *Times-Picayune* online." She walked to another window, agitated, gazing out into the city instead of at me. "You don't think you owe me an apology?"

"We never asked personal questions back then. I didn't ask who you were with outside of me and you never asked me. I always treated you well. I could apologize, but it would have no meaning," I said, firmly.

She crossed her arms protectively to snidely remark, "Oh, I'm not worthy of an apology because all we did was fuck?"

"We were enjoying each other's bodies and company. No strings, remember? I didn't lie to you. Every time I tried to bring up anything about our personal lives, you stopped me, remember? Don't rewrite history or play the victim now. That's the one thing I've always admired about you. You're a bad bitch and don't take shit off anyone." I held my hands up when her head whipped around, and said quickly, "And before you scratch my eyes out, I'm not calling you a bitch. Just simply stating a fact."

Royalty turned back to the window before she could hide her grin.

Wanting to keep her smiling, I cajoled, "You know you're still drawn to me, fuck, we're drawn to each other like moths to a flame. And I sure as hell don't care if I get burned, if it means I get a chance to be with you. We're amazing together. Last night proved that. We're both older now and I want to be with you."

She squinted her eyes at me. "Me and who else?"

I sighed. "I do deserve that, but I want only you. When I saw you again in the French Market, I felt like that man again, whose heart stopped at the sight of a beautiful woman with a body for days and a smart mouth I loved using my tongue to tame." Still nude, I moved to stand behind her, not yet touching. She had to bend to my will. I would only chase so much.

Hugging herself tighter, she said softly, "I figured you had a woman somewhere. You were too charming and sexy not to have some woman waiting anxiously for your call. Men like you always have a woman somewhere waiting."

Knowing her pride might prevent her from telling the truth, I still asked quietly, "Were you one of them?"

She pressed her forehead against the glass. "Yes. Much as I hate to admit it."

My heart soared at her genuine response. "And I always waited for your call, still waiting. I wished I'd met you first."

"Before your wife *and* your mistresses? I heard you couldn't stay faithful even after me."

Not to be deterred by her insistence of my horrible treatment of women, I said near her ear, "You are the only woman I've ever met who takes my breath away with just your mere presence, who not only stimulates but surpasses my intellect, my drive. I can't wait to see your face, hear your voice, just fucking be with you. No other woman matters more to me than you. And for the record, you were and are a better lover than any of them."

She shook her head. "Devin, you're so damn good at sweet talk. I can't make the same mistake and fall for you again. I was young and foolish then and settled for no strings, too scared to ask for more. Your whole vibe made it clear you only wanted one thing from me, no matter how many times you traveled to see me. And based on how we met, and that I let you get it from me within an hour of knowing you, I can't and don't really blame you. Last night was amazing and a short walk down memory lane. We got caught up in the romance of it all. Let's not make more of it than that."

Frustrated that she could diminish the magical time we'd shared, be so dismissive of my feelings, I growled, "I fucking told you I love you."

She twisted her neck to gaze into my eyes. "And I believe you, but to be with you is another story. You and I are not a good idea."

My eyes traveled her body, my dick stiff, knowing that one night would never be enough. "Then why haven't you walked away from me? I'm not holding you here."

Royalty dropped her gaze and turned her head away from me. "You're blocking my path."

"You can walk around me."

She quipped, "Back up first."

I smiled at her obvious weakness for me. "No."

Facing the window, she retorted, "Stop grinning like you won something."

"See, you already know me."

"I know you can't be trusted."

"The old me, yes. Getting a woman was always easy for me and I used them to stroke my ego. I promise I'm not that man anymore. I've learned...hell, I'm still learning from my mistakes." I placed my hands on the window, using my arms to block her in, still not touching her. "Tame me, Queen."

Royalty inhaled deeply, shoulders still rigid. "You said that I was your queen. Even though I knew it was a line, I loved whenever you called me that."

"It wasn't a line. You were and have always been my queen."

She shrugged her shoulders and replied drily, "If you say so."

I resisted the urge to groan in utter exasperation. "Royalty, can you honestly tell me that you never thought about me again?"

Royalty responded cautiously. "I did think of you."

"Then why is it impossible for me to never have thought of you even when I've been with other women?"

"I don't know. It's simply different with men. You can have sex with a woman for years and never take her seriously. We were only involved a few months a few days at a time, while you were married, *remember*? Why would I believe I was your queen then or now?"

"I can't change my past."

"I'm worried about the present and the future. You like the challenge of me. I become your woman, we have some fun, you get bored and it's on to your next challenge."

"I need a good woman to take care of me, be there for me, make me do right."

She snapped, "Wrong. You need to do right on your own."

Feeling her anger return, I covered her hands with my own, cajoling, "But it's so much more fun if you make me. I swear to you, I'm a one-woman man now. And this man wants you to be that woman."

She chuckled softly, the tenseness in her body ebbing slowly away. "A tad corny, don't you think?"

"You see, I can't run game with you. I never could. Any other woman would be melting and you still all heartless and cold."

She murmured, "I'm no different than any other woman when it comes to you. You could charm the pants off a lesbian."

I teased, "I did get Ellen's digits when she was in the city for a celebrity fundraiser for my father."

"You are horrible." Royalty laughed and her head fell against the top of my chest.

No longer able to resist the tempting smooth neck of Royalty, I placed my lips gently on her skin and I felt her slight shiver. "Spend the rest of the weekend with me. Let's go somewhere, take a drive, and eat dinner on the beach. I remember how much you missed water living in DC."

Royalty curved her body to mine, and my arms warmly embraced her. "I can't believe you remember that."

"We had good memories, let's make more."

"Devin..."

I tightened my arms. "No. I can't take you turning me down again. If we leave now, we can be at the beach in time for dinner. If you're not ready to believe I can be not only the man you want, but also the man you need, give me a chance to show you."

"Just the weekend. Monday, we return to our corners."

"If that's the way you want it," I agreed, determined to change her mind. She was destined to be my queen.

14

DEVIN

Sheltered in my arms on a blanket while we enjoyed the cool breeze of the water off the Gulf of Mexico, after a dinner of fried lobsters and Greek salads, I bared my soul to Royalty. I wanted her to understand me, my faults, my weaknesses, my strengths. Everything.

"After my marriage ended, I had to do some serious soul searching, self-reflection. I'd lost everything. My wife, my daughter, and temporarily, my father. He had lost the election to Tre and he blamed me for it. Because he'd been too afraid to admit that Tre had been the better candidate for mayor, he said that the scandal of my divorce made voters leery to vote for him. I stayed away from my family, even Nicholas, nursing my wounds, trying to get a handle on my life and where I went wrong. I even searched for you on the internet and found out that you were a lawyer at a firm in New Orleans. I started to reach out and then stopped myself because I was not in a good emotional space. You were the one woman I thought I didn't hurt, and I wanted it to stay that way.

"The first clear memory of my parents had to be when I was five years old. My parents had gotten into a huge argument because I told my mother that my dad and I visited one of his lady friends. I didn't know that this friend had been one of his lovers. My mother left our home angry and my father beat me and warned me to never open my mouth about him again. He rarely hit me, but when he did, it was pretty bad, and my mother would have to intervene for him to stop."

"Was he abusive to your mother too?"

I hugged her tighter, thinking about the relationship I had with my father as a boy. "Until you asked me that question, I didn't see his treatment of me as abuse. I was stubborn, always had a smart mouth, wanted things my way. I wasn't an easy child to raise. His sometimes harsh treatment of me was deserved, or at least that's what I told myself, because he wasn't that way with my mother. He never hit her, or if he did, I never saw any evidence of it."

"He made you feel that you deserved his punishments. I mean, what five-year-old child would lie to his mother about how he spent his day?"

"Yeah...well, for a long time I refused to go anywhere with him. Only wanted to be around my mother, and of course that further damaged our relationship since I was his only child, his only son." I stared into the ocean, thinking about our turbulent relationship over the years. "The last time my father hit me, I was sixteen. We had words about how he was treating my mother, and he punched me hard in the chest when I got in his face. I'd grown taller than him, and I pushed him so hard he lost his balance and fell. I ran out of the house and jumped in my car, deciding to leave home once and for all. I used to race my Mustang on Haynes, so I headed there to win cash until I could figure out my next step.

"I pulled up to the crowd that gathered on the stretch of road near the levee to watch cars race. Police would be called on occasion, but for the most part no one cared about this road behind a black neighborhood. I'd been careful in the past about who I raced. I never wanted to go against the drug dealers who used to frequent the area, too. That day I didn't care, and I beat this guy who ran with Blue St. John's crew. He was pissed because a rich boy beat him, and instead of giving me money, he pulled a gun on me. Everyone scattered and the street cleared in seconds. Already still hurt from the fight with my father, I didn't back down, didn't care if he killed me—until this huge man with dreadlocks came out of nowhere and ordered the dude to put his gun down."

※

THE TALL AND THICK MAN WITH TATTS COVERING HIS NECK repeated, "Put the gun down now, Tricks, or deal with me later."

I stood in the middle of the street, fists balled, waiting to meet my maker. I didn't have anything to live for. My father hated me, and deep down I believed my mother would always side with him over me.

The young guy tightened his grip on the gun. "You don't think I'm going to pull the trigger?"

I snapped back, "I don't give a fuck if you do or not. Go ahead and pull it."

He moved closer, the gun aimed at my head, obviously trying to punk me. I ignored the gun and stared at the boy, who was probably my age. I saw movement from the corner of my eye, and the man had moved behind him and grabbed him around the neck. He pushed the arm that held the gun away from me. It went off, and the bullet hit the driver's side of my car. The trigger boy's eyes widened, and he dropped the gun, which the big man deftly picked up and aimed at him.

The young man put his arms up, slowly backing away. "Come on, Deaux. I was just trying to scare him."

He growled, "What did I tell you to do? Huh?"

Real fear crossed his countenance at the menacing glare in the man called Deaux's eyes. "You told me to put the gun down."

"What else did I fucking say?"

His voice trembled. "Deal with you later."

He cocked the gun. "Did you follow orders?"

I stared in fascination at the scene unfolding before me. Death seemed imminent for the young soldier in the streets of New Orleans.

"Honor your word and give the man his money."

The teen kept one arm up while reaching in his pocket and tossed a wad of money at my feet.

Deaux said, "Give Blue a direct message—that you're not allowed back on this strip, and that you're lucky Deaux didn't kill your punk ass."

The guy nodded and ran to his car and within seconds left with a squeal of tires in the opposite direction.

Deaux slipped the gun in the back waistband of his jeans. He then went to the side of my car and kneeled to check the hole. "I can fix this. Bring it by my shop."

Now that the danger had passed and my adrenaline rush gone, all that remained was pain. Leaving the money, I walked numbly to my car and watched as this man who saved my life, who seemed so calm, stood and reached in his pocket to give me a card. I didn't look at him as I took the card because I had already starting crying and couldn't face this strong man in the middle of my weakness.

"Thank you," I mumbled.

Before I could turn away, he did the strangest thing. He embraced me. At first my arms went limp, wondering his angle. I'd never been hugged by another man, not even my father. He held on and said, "Let go, young soldier, let go."

Then I grabbed on to him tight and cried for all the pain and hurt I had bottled inside of me. Afterwards, we sat on the curb, in the middle of the night, and I confided in a perfect stranger about the fight I had with my father and how all I ever wanted was to have my father's love and respect. He told me he ran the streets to gain the respect of his father, who had already been killed in the very same streets.

"It's insanity to try to be our fathers or what we perceive our fathers want us to be. Be you. Always be you. Maybe your pops will respect you, maybe he won't. But you will always respect yourself as long as you're being true to self."

"Why did you step in and save me?" I asked him.

"This is a safe space for everyone. Blue asked me to watch over it. No drug or gang wars. No violence of any kind is allowed. I had to protect it." He gave me a grudging smile. "You would have made a good soldier. You didn't back down and focused on his eyes and not his gun."

"Honestly, I didn't care if I lived or died."

"You remained in your truth at that moment, which is why you had no fear. And now, do you care if you live or die?"

"I do care. I have a lot to live for." I swallowed the lump in my throat as I considered how close I'd come to death.

"Then go back home and figure this out with your pops. If you can't then call me. Remember that you stared down a bullet with your name on it tonight and survived. Live in your truth. You have a lot of heart, Devin, and no one can take that from you."

"I only survived because of you."

"Naw, he wouldn't have pulled the trigger once he saw you weren't scared. You punked him. The gun went off because he was surprised by me. I had to get the gun from him to make a point. He won't be back, and if he sees you in another part of the city, he's going to pretend he ain't never met you. You good."

"How can you be so sure?"

Deaux simply stood up, dusted off his jeans, and went to pick up the cash. "Bring your car to my shop and I'll fix it." He handed me my winnings. "If you need money, you can help around the shop."

"I WENT HOME IN THE WEE HOURS OF THE MORNING. My parents were still awake in the great room, and both looked like they had been crying. My mother rushed to me and hugged me. My father remained seated, but I read the apology in his eyes. I nodded and smelled my mother's familiar flowery scent. Glad to be home. My father never touched me again in anger, and our relationship became somewhat easier. Not the way I would like us to be, but enough that we could tolerate each other until I moved out when I headed to college."

"Your parents had no idea that they almost lost their son forever. I can't believe that's how you met Mr. Deaux. I assumed you got into some trouble like shoplifting or something and you were sent to work for him."

"Shoplifting?"

She kissed my chin and looked up at me. "Not saying I think you used to be a thief...okay, maybe stealing girls' hearts...but not a real thief."

"You have jokes."

"Seriously, Mr. Deaux always had some young men at the shop, and he always made sure that Raini and I kept our distance because he was overprotective, so I never really knew who they were or how they ended up working with him."

"He had a mix of young men, some of us with no record who needed guidance, and then some who had records as long as my arm. I worked off the damage to my car. And even after I'd more than paid for the damages, I went to his shop after school and on weekends. I felt peace in his presence, something that I never experienced with my own father. Sometimes we would have deep discussions about the plight of black men, the black community, and other times we would joke around, and he would tease me about the girls who were always blowing up my cell. I remember seeing Raini a couple of times at the shop, but she was a little girl, so I didn't look at her as anything other than Deaux's daughter."

I put one arm around Royalty's neck, holding her to me. "I remember when the local Baton Rouge news announced Deaux's death, and a part of me died. My college apartment was only a few miles from where he was killed. I drove by the shop whose front window had been boarded the next day, and I kept wishing I could turn back time so I could save him like he saved me, but he was already gone. I swear to you, I grieved him like my own blood. He had become a father to me, and his death was a blow I don't think I ever fully recovered from."

"I'm still trying to wrap my head around the fact that we both knew and loved the same man. Now I understand why Mr. Deaux means so much to you and why Raini has a soft spot for you." She snuggled deeper into my arms

"Yeah, I had no idea that she planned to give me her garter. That was a stroke of genius on her part. Hate that I didn't think of it."

"Umm...hmmm. Lucky I think you're so fucking sexy, or I would have to kill her when she gets back from her honeymoon." She undulated her hips and my dick stirred.

"Queen, I need you to stop moving before I take you on this beach. I still have more to say, and your luscious ass is distracting me."

She groaned seductively. "Okay, I'll stop for now. Something about not backing down to a gun just increased your hot factor."

"Only a woman would find that hot."

"Yep, please continue talking so you can take me on this beach like you just threatened."

I looked at the calm waters of the Gulf to rein my body back in, because she needed to understand me before we moved forward. "I used my grief as motivation to finish college and then my law degree, wanting to help men like Deaux who rarely get a fair chance in the criminal justice system. I accepted an internship under Nia's dad to better understand policy. He was completely different from my father and Deaux. His demeanor serious, reserved, his intelligence crazy high, and he loved his wife and daughter. He became my mentor and took me under his wing, sharing ideas and thoughts about law, politics, and life. Nia had been away for school initially, and when she returned, she kept her distance from me at first. Then she began dating Tre, my best friend at the time.

I'd been enjoying the single life, no thoughts of getting married anytime soon, when he noticed us talking at his birthday party. He suggested I bring Nia to hear one of his lectures. We ended up having a good time and had engaging conversation. Nia wanted to spend more time together, and her father openly preferred me to Tre, anyway, telling me that it was time for me to settle down. He said if I wanted longevity in politics, I needed to find a suitable wife.

"I began to look at Nia differently and realized that she wasn't like the women I had dated. She didn't care about my money or my family's influence and seemed to like me for me. And deep down we both wanted to please her father. Neither one of us knew how to tell Tre. A part of me felt like he wasn't that serious about her and wasn't ready to settle down yet. I thought that once he knew, he would be mad for a little while but then get over it. But he didn't. I lost my best friend, but I gained a wife and a family.

"I'd only been married a few months when I met you. I wasn't looking for anyone, hadn't cheated on my wife, though I already had doubts about my marriage. Realizing that I'd gotten myself into a situation, I was afraid I couldn't get out. I thought having her in my life would suddenly make that void, that emptiness that had been left by Deaux, go away, but it didn't until you."

Twisting her head to meet my eyes, she asked, "Really?"

"Yes." I bent my head and gently kissed her. Her hands curved backward around my neck, and she flicked her tongue in my mouth for a tantalizing second. "You were so unexpected. Believe it or not, I'd never had sex so fast with a woman. It was crazy how instant our attraction was, the chemistry between us.

I swallowed my guilt by justifying my behavior. I attributed my infidelity to being away from home and that I had a momentary lapse in judgment. I promised myself that it wouldn't happen again. Except once I returned home, I couldn't get you out of my mind. I had to see you again, devised this whole elaborate lie that I had a project in DC to excuse my absences from home. No one knew about you. People would comment about how happy I seemed, and that marriage must agree with me, but the truth of the matter was, it was you. Every time I left you, especially because you never expected me or asked when I would return, I swore it was the last time. I was like this lovesick puppy, irritable when I couldn't see you, happy when I did. Nia was just getting to know me as her husband, and I didn't make it easy for her because I felt trapped. I wanted out of the marriage, but I didn't see how that was possible at the time. By the third month of seeing you, I was ready to confess and hope that you could forgive me. I wanted you to know the truth."

I could feel her body stiffening in my arms. "So, I could be your side piece willingly?"

"Honestly, I don't know what I expected or wanted from you. I just wanted to tell you everything and we would take it from there. But you made it clear you didn't want to know anything about my love life."

"You could've tried harder."

"Queen, you know I tried, and every time you shut me down. I thought then that maybe you didn't feel like I did, and so what was the point of telling you if you only saw me as a fun time."

"You broke my heart because I saw you as more than that. I wanted more, and the day I sent you the text that I didn't want to see you again...I...I..." She suddenly stood and moved closer to the water's edge and looked up at the sky. I remained sitting, sensing she needed space. "I found out...I found out that..."

"You found out I was married. I know that now, and I hate that you didn't find out from me."

She hugged herself.

I ached to hold her, make her feel better. I could see the pain in her stance. "Nicholas told me that was probably the reason you shut me out, and I didn't believe him. Didn't think you cared enough to look into my life."

Royalty turned around, angry. "I loved you. But what type of future did I have with a newly married man?"

"I'd fallen for you, too. How I wished we had talked back then."

"For what? For us to have this forbidden love behind the scenes. Because you sure as hell weren't leaving your wife at the height of your and her family's political career."

"Maybe I would have if I'd known the woman who could make my heart sing with just the sound of her voice loved me too."

"You just said you didn't know how it was possible to leave her."

Barely able to control my frustration at her unwillingness to believe she meant the world to me then, I acknowledged sharply, "I know what I said."

Royalty clasped her hands together tightly and bit out, "What about the other affairs, the other women? People talk."

I shut my eyes to the pain of losing her, because she was slowly withdrawing from me. Could I blame her? Why would she put her precious heart in my dirty hands? For a long time, I didn't give a fuck that I hurt my ex-wife, and it was coming back to haunt me.

"There was only one other woman besides you. Yeah, I flirted a lot, stayed out late at the bars and clubs when I should have been home with my wife. I didn't want to be at home because I couldn't be with you, the woman I really loved. I didn't cheat on Nia again until we struggled to conceive. I thought having a child would fix me, take away this damn void left by the lack of my father's love, the death of Deaux, and then you ending our relationship. When we tried for two painful years and nothing happened, I started seeing a woman I used to date in college." I picked up a pebble and threw it far, dreading the next part of the conversation. "I don't know how much you heard, but there's something else you should know."

Royalty looked back at me, scowl in place. "What?"

"The other woman was Nia's best friend."

15

DEVIN

Chuckling sardonically, she said, "I keep asking God for a man who lights my heart afire, who makes me smile just being in his presence, that fills my soul with joy... and then I get you. You make me feel all these things, but maybe I'm such a fool in love with you, I'm blind to my own gut instincts that you're bad for me. A man who would stoop so low to sleep with his wife's best friend. From what I hear, your ex-wife is one of the sweetest, caring women. Cheating on her is horrible enough, but with her best friend, Devin? Her best friend? You obviously don't know the meaning of friendship, of honor, of respect, of trust, of love, and definitely not loyalty."

Her words were icicles stabbing every part of me, but I had to take whatever she said. I wanted to yell that Melanie only became friends with Nia to still be in my life. That I didn't even know about their friendship until I stopped by my wife's job to pick her up. That I had been pissed that she'd manipulated her way back into my life, and I ignored Mel for years until I didn't. That I'd attempted to atone for my sins by being faithful and committed to my marriage after a brief separation, once my wife returned to me pregnant with another man's child. That I'd willingly accepted my wife's love child as my own because Nia deserved more than I'd ever given her. I wanted to say all those things, but instead I spoke the plain truth. "There's no justification for my behavior."

"No, there isn't." She shivered.

I stood, dusting the sand off my trousers. I picked up the blanket and placed it around her shoulders. "Cold?" I placed my hands in my pockets to stop myself from touching her again.

Royalty looked at me, hurt and sadness written all over her face. "No. Trying to wrap my head around being with a man who would do that to his wife. That's the ultimate betrayal. Maybe if you were still with this woman, then you could say it was about love. But you can't even say that. What happened with her?"

"We dated briefly during my divorce, but I wasn't in the space to be with anyone. I was depressed, angry, grieving, hurt that I'd lost a child I thought I would raise. I'd became irrational, even contemplated fighting Nia for custody, using whatever means or legal actions I could think of to fight for a child who wasn't biologically mine."

Royalty's head jerked up. "You tried to get custody of Nya?"

I moved to stand in front of her, hoping she would look at me, remember that she loves me. "I told you I was irrational. Much as I hate to admit it, Nya's father has more power and influence than me. Since you seem to know so much about me, I'm sure you've heard she's with Justin Ray."

Staring past my shoulder, Royalty commented, "So, if he wasn't one of the biggest entertainers in the world, you would've tried to take Nia's baby away from her."

"The way I felt at that time, I would have pursued it. I couldn't grasp the unfairness of it all, that I could lose a child just like that. That the love I poured into that little girl meant nothing because my wife decided she didn't want to be with me anymore. I'd never felt more powerless in my life. And being with Mel just reminded me of how fucked up I'd been as a husband, as a man. She reminded me that I'd become my father and repeated his callous treatment of my mother. As time passed, I finally let go of my anger and focused on being a better man."

Only the sounds of the waves rolling in and out drifted between us as I stared down at the silent, brooding woman capable of forever crippling me if she walked away from us. I picked up her cool hand and placed it on my cheek. "Please, I don't want to lose you again."

Royalty's eyes softened as she finally met my intense, pleading gaze. She asked quietly, "When's the last time you saw her?"

Refusing to ever lie to her again, I admitted, "I hadn't seen Mel in two years, until last night. She was with her new man at the reception."

Although her breathing quickened, she gave a subtle nod. "Did it bother you seeing her with someone?"

Taking her hand off my cheek to press against my heart, I reassured her, "I felt nothing when I saw her or her new man. She still seemed salty even with her new love, but I didn't care. You were my focus."

"Did you promise her that you would marry her once you ended your marriage?"

"No, but I knew she believed that it would happen. It was what she'd hoped for, what she'd schemed for. We were duplicitous together, and maybe we deserved one another at some point. But becoming a father changed me. Made me wake up to the reality that I wanted my child to be proud of me, and I'd been doing whatever the fuck I wanted, hurting people left and right, because *I* was hurt, uncaring as long as I got what I wanted. And losing Nya was my punishment."

Royalty tapped her hand against my chest and demanded, "Why are you telling me all this?"

I tugged her even closer. "Because I need you to trust me."

"What difference does it matter if I trust you or not when I'm not sure we should be together?"

Unwilling to be denied a second chance, I grabbed her face

with both my hands and kissed her surprisingly pliant lips. When she moaned, I broke the kiss to whisper hoarsely, "I want you to be my wife."

Royalty stared at me, eyes wide, searching my face for lies, the truth, probably all of the above. She inhaled deeply before speaking. "I do love you, but you're not the marrying kind. Women are drawn to you, and your flesh is too weak. There's nothing wrong with being single and enjoying being with women. Then you never have to worry about breaking another woman's heart or feeling guilt, regret, and shame about what you did."

I gritted my teeth. "Do you want a husband?"

She frowned. "Of course, I do."

"Why?"

Her response was quick. "My parents have been married forever. They've had their arguments, but the love between them is so deep, I never worried that their fights would last. They are partners for life. My father considers my mother above all else before making decisions, and my mother knows when to follow him blindly or stand up to him. I am strong-willed and stubborn, but I have absolutely no problem submitting to a man who I know will always lead me correctly. To know that there is another soul that genuinely loves, understands, and accepts me is priceless, and I'm perfectly fine being single until I find that in a man. I want him to be my head of household, and I'll be his backbone. Our family can't function successfully without the other."

Needing her to believe me, I wrapped my arms around her and implored, "I love you and I want that type of life partnership. Do you want me as your husband?"

Royalty sighed, "Devin..."

"Answer from your heart, not your mind, or what I just told you, or your fears of me hurting you."

Her body quivered and she gazed into my eyes. Two tears

dropped slowly onto her cheek. "You feel so meant for me, it's unreal."

I tilted her chin so she could see me. Really see the man I'd become. The one meant to be her husband. "Then I want to start with your heart."

"I don't know...this weekend was unbelievably romantic until now, but..."

"No buts...it's just you and me. We can figure it out. I'm an open book now. If I do anything that you don't like or makes you distrust me, tell me. I'll give you a key to my house, my cars, my passwords to my cell, my laptop...whatever you need to feel safe me with me. No rush to make any decisions. I just need a chance to prove to you I can be the man you desire."

"It's not just me...I have a son," she said quietly, again studying my expression, waiting for my reaction.

Not expecting her admission, my heart pounded in confusion. "A son? With that man? How old?"

She trembled in my arms as she responded in a rush, "Yes. No. His dad is not involved, and he's young—too young to be around you if you and I are not solid. Are you okay with dating me, knowing that I have a child? Are you ready for fatherhood?"

Closing my eyes tight, I tried to digest this new information. I'd never pictured her as a mother. Her body hadn't changed much, and she didn't have the telltale signs of stretch marks. Was I ready to be a father to a child who wasn't mine again?

"Is he the reason you've been running from me...the man you have waiting at home for you?"

"Yes." She suddenly averted her gaze. "Anthony's someone I've been dating, but we're not serious. I only pretended we were in a relationship to keep you away because I didn't know how you would feel about me being a mother." Royalty shivered again and I rubbed her arms, trying to determine my own feelings. "Raini babysits a lot, and I have a stand-by sitter when she can't, which is a lot lately since she's with Tre now. So, if we do this, know that I can't be at your beck and call. And that eventually if everything is good between us, you and he will meet."

"I...don't know what to say." I whistled, trying to ease the throbbing in my head. "There's still a hole in my heart from Nya. I don't know if I can take getting close to another child and know I could possibly lose them, too."

"Have you changed your mind about us?" Her voice was barely a whisper over the sounds of the waves.

Realizing Royalty had taken my words as a shift in my desires, instead of processing my thoughts and emotions out loud, I wiped the wetness from her cheeks before speaking. "Queen, I haven't changed my mind, just needed a moment to process everything. I told you that I can't lose you again, so let's take it slow, and one day we'll both be ready for me to meet your son."

I rubbed her back, rocking her as she cried in my chest. I had more questions about her life and the man who left her to raise her child alone, but I sensed she wasn't yet ready to talk. I looked up in the clear starry night, the moon a perfect crescent, and prayed that God could finally forgive me for my sins by granting me the forever love of one Royalty James.

16

ROYALTY

Devin asked, "Did you like the purse?"

"You didn't get my voicemail message?" I propped my bare feet on my desk and adjusted my wireless earbuds to hear him better. "When I saw that gorgeous Hermès bag on the table in my office, I screamed so loud, my paralegal thought I'd lost my mind. I absolutely love it!"

I could hear the smile in his voice. "I saw you eyeing it at the mall."

"It's so expensive, baby." Leaning back in my chair, I commented, "You do know the way we both love to shop, we'll be completely broke before the year is over."

"You're with me now, whatever you want, I got you," he boasted.

"You really like spoiling me."

"You're my queen." Devin then said in a lower voice, "Let me take care of you...like later tonight."

I pouted. "I can't, baby. It's a school night."

"I can wait until Ryder's asleep and sneak out before he wakes up."

"You are way too loud for us to be down the hall from him."

Devin chuckled. "I can't argue with the truth."

"Besides, we will have the whole weekend to ourselves when he goes with Tre and Raini to Disneyworld." They'd offered to bring Ryder on their family trip so that I could spend time with Devin and tell him the truth about our son. Tre had pieced together that Ryder was Devin's son the last time Ryder spent the day with them, and he'd been upset that Devin still didn't know.

"Come on, Queen, it's been almost two months. If Tre can take him on a family trip, why can't I meet him? Just introduce us so he can get used to me being around. He's going to be my son sooner or later."

I quickly looked around my home office as if Ryder, who was in his room on the other side of the house, could hear Devin. I'd planned to tell Devin the truth that night on the beach, especially after he opened up to me about his life, but I could still hear the bitterness in his voice about losing Nya. If Devin seriously contemplated pursuing custody for a child who wasn't biologically his, he was more than capable of taking Ryder from me if our relationship didn't work.

That night I decided that I would treat Devin like any other man I'd dated, and that I needed more time to solidify us before introducing Ryder to him. "And he didn't spend time with Tre until he and Raini had been together for months. I promise that you will meet Ryder soon."

He sighed in disappointment. "Alright. Lunch tomorrow at my office?"

"Of course. I'll pick up some gumbo for us on my way there."

Devin quickly protested, "No, I'll have it delivered. Your lunch break is too short for us to waste precious time when you could be in my arms."

"Why are you so damn sweet?" I gushed.

"You make it easy. I'll call you before I go to sleep."

"Okay." I clicked off my cell and held the phone against my chest, marveling at the depth of emotions we felt for one another. Loving Devin felt like an exhilarating thrill ride. The anticipation of seeing him, being with him, leaving him with the excitement, joy, hope, and expectation that I get to do it all over again.

We spent our days and nights either texting or calling each other. I promised to have lunch with him every day since our offices were not far from each other. He preferred we meet at his office instead of restaurants, so we could get in a quickie when the mood hit. I enjoyed meeting each member of his firm and appreciated the laid-back manner in which he and his team worked. If I didn't think we would kill each other with too much togetherness, our heated varying opinions, or plain stubbornness, I might consider working with him.

For now, I enjoyed the giddiness of lost and found love, knowing that now Devin was mine and only mine, a feeling I wasn't quite ready to let go, afraid that everything would change once I told him about Ryder.

Ryder knocked before he peeked his head in my office, interrupting my thoughts. "Grammy on the phone. She wants to speak to you, too."

I whispered, "Tell her I'll call her back."

"I can hear you. Talk to me now," my mother responded crisply.

"You should have told me she was on speaker." I gave Ryder the evil eye as he passed me the phone.

"Grammy, Mama is mad with me." He laughed as he ducked, anticipating my swat at his head.

She complained, "You're always too busy to talk to me."

"I'm too busy period, Mama."

"We don't see you and the baby often. At the very least we should talk more."

"Ryder is almost eleven. He hates when you refer to him as a baby."

"We only see you once a year, and if we're lucky twice, so I still think of him as my sweet chocolate grandbaby."

"That's the life of the military that you and Dad and my brother seem to love so much. We are here and you can visit us at any time."

"That's why I'm calling. We want you and Ryder to travel to Okinawa for a couple of weeks during the summer. Your father is finishing up a project, and he can't take that much time off."

Being without Devin for two weeks had already become unthinkable. Crazy how he had become such a part of me in a short period of time. "Would it be okay if I brought a friend with us?"

"Raini is still a newlywed...you must be talking about a man."

"Yes. We're serious about each other, and he wants to marry me." I figured I would start out with the good news first. My mother has wanted me to be married, almost more than she wanted me to be a lawyer.

"Of course, he does! Who wouldn't want to marry you? Who is he?" Although my mother could annoy the hell out of me and had been tough on me, even more than my father about being an unwed mother, she never missed an opportunity to remind me of my worth.

"He's a lawyer and his father used to be the mayor of New Orleans."

"Derrick Toussaint?"

"Yes. His son's name is Devin."

She clapped her hands. "Jackpot, Royalty! Told you to not give up."

I rolled my eyes. "No, you told me I was too picky."

"You are, but if you're with this man, your pickiness paid off. Does Ry like him?"

"Haven't introduced them yet."

"If you're serious, then you need to let them meet. Boys can be tough on their mother's suitors."

"Trust me, I know. I plan to let them meet soon." I stood and quietly closed the door, not wanting Ryder to accidentally hear the next part of my news to my mother. "It doesn't really matter if Ryder is tough on him or not because Devin is his father."

"His father?" I swear my mother's voice went up an octave. "Why on Earth are you just sharing this information? And why hasn't he been involved all this time?"

"Long story short, because I didn't plan to tell you this right now. We had an affair. I didn't know he had a wife until I got pregnant. I immediately ended with him and never told him about Ryder because I didn't want to spend my life being the outside family. He's divorced now and we have rekindled a real relationship this time."

"How does he feel about Ryder?"

"He doesn't know yet. I only told him I have a son, and that one day soon he and Ry will meet."

Silence on the other end.

"Say whatever you need to say, Mama. I know you're probably disappointed in me yet again. I didn't know he was married. I swear to you."

"You've always had a strong mind and will, and I told you that once you became an adult, I would step back and you could make any decisions that you want. And that you would have to live with the consequences of your choices, good or bad. Did I not say that?"

"Yes, ma'am. But you made me feel like I had messed up my life, like all I had accomplished went away because I got pregnant."

"I have never been disappointed in you. You graduated college and just started law school before you had a child. You've always been resourceful and bright, and it shows in how you're raising Ryder, a son with whom you've done a good job—not just as a single mother, but a parent, period. You've created a full life for you and him mostly by yourself. Yes, I told you, you were on your own when you first told me about Ry. Me and your daddy had already made plans to travel with his work, and we weren't going to change them for our grown daughter who decided to become a mother without benefit of a husband. No judgment, Royal, just facts.

"I was there when you gave birth and stayed with you two months after that, but the rest was up to you. If you took our decision to continue to live our lives as a sign that we were disappointed in you, you were wrong. My tone and my questions may have been sharp over the years, but that was only out of worry and concern because I knew it would be and has been tough. My tone and questions were never because I was ever ashamed or disappointed. How could I be, when I love you and Ryder so much?"

It was my turn to be silent.

"I can't tell you I would have made a different decision than you when you first found out you were pregnant and that Devin had a wife, because it didn't happen to me. The one thing I can say is that you need to tell him sooner rather than later, because it will be a shock to him and Ryder, and there may be anger and hurt directed at you from both of them. They've waited long enough to meet. Has this man been good to you so far?"

I answered without reservation, "Yes, the best."

"Then you and he will be able to get past this. I look forward to meeting Devin, and he is welcome to come with you and Ry. You probably have to go, but when you have more time, I would like to know more about your new man and about Raini's wedding. I hate we missed it."

I pushed my papers to the side and propped my knees against my desk. "I have time now, Mama. And even if Devin can't make the trip, Ry and I will be there. We would love to visit Japan. How's my daddy?"

"Missing you and Ry. He wanted me to wait to talk to you once he made it back home."

"I miss you and Daddy so much. We can just FaceTime him tomorrow so we can see both of you. Tell me about Okinawa."

"It's so beautiful here..."

Holding the phone between my ear and shoulder, I listened

to my mother speak animatedly about her home for the past six months. I had been wrong about her, even avoided her phone calls at times because I feared her judgment, and the more time I spent with Devin, the more I wondered if I had misjudged him, as well.

17

ROYALTY

As soon as I dropped off Ryder at Tre and Raini's house, I headed to Devin's place Thursday night. We'd both taken off Friday and spent the whole day in bed watching movies and eating junk food.

After a dinner of fried shrimp po' boys and fries we had delivered, I tapped his firm belly. "We can't have too many days like this, if you want to keep looking like this."

He gripped my thigh. "I like this fullness on you. It's me and you from here on out, so we will look out for each other, making sure we don't go too far since we both love to eat. Of course, you can always work up a sweat fucking my brains out."

"I have to keep my hair braided or weaved around you, or I'll never keep my hair tamed with all the sweating we do whenever we're around each other."

Devin tugged on one of my long twists. "As long as you give me something to pull on when I'm hitting it from the back, I don't care what hairstyle you rock."

I rolled on top of his naked body. "Good thing I'm just as sex crazed as you, or I would think you only want my body."

He cupped my face. "I want all of you forever."

I averted my eyes, hating that I kept prolonging the truth.

Devin lifted my face and forced me to look at him. "Hey, what's wrong?"

My heart thudded. "Thinking it's time for you to meet Ryder." There, I said it. The first step.

"Okay," he said carefully, his eyes never leaving mine. "I'm ready to meet him. Why the long face?"

I swallowed back the fear that lodged in my throat. "Scared to lose us," I said quietly.

"Why would we lose us?"

"Children have a way of changing dynamics."

He frowned. "I'm not a young man anymore. I expect most women around my age to have children. I know I have to share you."

"But you haven't dated any women with children before or after your marriage."

He shifted to lay on his side, and I faced him. "Before my marriage I wasn't ready to be a father or share my woman with anyone. After my divorce, I was too scared to get attached to someone's child. With you it's different. I want a life with you, and I get the bonus of having a son, who I hope to meet one day, since you won't tell me anything about him except his name."

"Can I have this weekend with just you? We haven't had any uninterrupted time alone since we got together." My instinct told me that we would argue because he'd want to know why I waited so long, and then he would take it as proof that I didn't trust him.

"Whatever you want. I'm not going anywhere." He looked at me, his forehead wrinkled. "Nothing is going to change between us, okay?"

My heart full, I offered, "I want to cook dinner at my home next week, and then you can meet Ryder."

His face relaxed into a smile. "It's time for the two men in your life to meet."

I pressed my lips against his. "Yes, past time for the two loves of my life to meet."

THE NEXT DAY I WAS RECLINING IN HIS MEDIA ROOM watching *A Bronx Tale* when Devin called. "I told you I could get us a free meal."

He had to run to his office and pick up some files. On the way back he stopped to pick up Italian I had delivered but the restaurant messed up the order.

"What did you promise?"

"That's not important. Point is, I handled what you couldn't."

"Did you get extra dressing and breadsticks?"

He chuckled, "The manager was a woman, I have enough bread for three meals."

The doorbell rang.

"You're expecting company?"

"I forgot the opposing counsel has a courier dropping off papers. I'm almost home. Don't open the door naked."

"I'll have you know I put on some clothes after you left."

"You probably only wearing my robe. Too lazy to get dressed."

I looked down at his robe, smiling at his accurate assessment. "Just get your ass home so you can see if I'm telling the truth."

"You're wearing my robe." He clicked off the phone.

Laughing, I opened the door without looking through the peephole. A woman with long black hair, wearing a tight dress and heels, stood at the door, hands on her hips and an ugly scowl on her pretty face. She raised one perfectly waxed eyebrow and asked snidely, "Why are you here?"

Did this random woman just address me like she knows me? Trying to hold my crazy at bay, I asked politely through clenched teeth, "I'm sorry, I don't believe we ever met. Can I help you?"

She crossed her arms. "Is Devin home?"

I gripped the knob. "No. Did he expect you?"

"No, but he told me I could drop by anytime."

I nodded, like her words didn't bother me, especially because he had told me the same thing. Hand on one hip, I said, "Maybe he did in the past, but I'm here now, and we expect a call before a visitor just drops by."

"*We?*" She looked me up and down with the left side of her lip curled in disdain.

"Did I stutter? *We* would prefer that if you want to stop by and see him, you call first."

She jerked her head back. "Oh, you're supposed to be his new woman?"

I slammed and locked the door, refusing to entertain this woman any longer.

She began to bang on the door and scream profanities. She was so loud I wouldn't doubt the neighbors heard.

I picked up my cell and called Devin.

He answered, "Hey, I'm pulling up."

"I want you to hear something." I turned the phone toward the door so he could hear the craziness.

"What the fuck?"

"Exactly." I clicked off the phone.

Seconds later, his car tires squealed in the driveway. A door slammed, and then I heard raised voices.

Hurrying to the window, I watched Devin and this stranger yelling at each other. I couldn't understand what they were saying because their voices were muffled. Although the woman's light-skinned face flushed red with anger, I saw the tears that threatened to fall.

Who was she to him? He had given me free rein in his home for the almost two months we'd been dating. Even if he wasn't home, he liked me to be waiting for him. Sometimes, because I couldn't stay the night, I would stop by, cook him dinner, and then go to my house. I hadn't seen any evidence of a woman since we'd been together, until now. Whoever she was, he had hurt her.

She smacked him hard across the face, and I flinched. He furiously lunged for her and she managed to evade his grasp, throwing him off balance. The woman then reared her hand back, ready to hit him again. Without thinking, I rushed out the door and shoved her away from him before she struck again. She staggered back, eyes wide.

Devin quickly jumped in between us and placed me behind him. "Mel, leave us alone. We've been over. Just go home."

Mel? His former mistress? The fuck?

Teeth bared, she yelled, "Why are you lying to her? You were just with me."

He gripped my wrist and stopped me from leaving or responding. "*When* were we together? Huh? Tell her when, so she can see you are a fucking liar."

"You're the fucking liar. Promised to be with me as soon as you left Nia. You're free now and have the nerve to parade this woman in front of me at the mayor's wedding, like I don't have feelings." Beneath the anger, her voice vibrated with pain.

She tried to come around him to hit me, but Devin wisely maneuvered me out of her path. If she got anywhere near me, I swear she would be on the ground.

"Mel, I'm calling the police if you don't leave," Devin warned.

Mel yelled over his shoulder, "You're just the next bitch in line."

Her words fueled my anger, as I taunted, "And you were the last bitch, so the fuck what?"

She lunged at me, and I tried to shove Devin out of the way to get to her, but he pushed me toward the door. "Go back inside. I got this."

Livid that I had to even deal with this reality TV bullshit, I rushed back inside and grabbed my keys and my purse. I didn't care that all I wore was his robe. When I hurried to my car, Mel raced after me again, but Devin grabbed her arm and stopped her.

"You better run, bitch," she sneered.

I thought about knocking her down on her prissy, backstabbing ass. Instead, I jumped in my car and started the ignition.

"Where are you going?" Devin yelled. He let go of Mel and jumped in front of my car. "Get out of the car, Royalty."

I pressed the window down "I swear to God, I will run you over. Get the fuck out of my way!"

Mel had a smirk on her face. "Let her leave."

"You going to have to hit me, because I'm not moving."

I revved the engine, but he didn't budge. I screamed in frustration and hit the steering wheel. I couldn't hurt him.

Devin yanked open my door. "You're not leaving me over some past bullshit. I can't live without you, do you understand that? Do you get you're my world now?"

Tears rained down my face. "She better be the past. I can't...I can't." I choked over my words.

He kneeled by my side, his eyes red, wiping my face. "I swear to you, I'm not that man anymore. I only want you, will always only want and love you."

Mel threw a rock that bounced off the side of my car and barely missed Devin's head. He jumped up and charged her. His sudden and quick movements forced her to run from him. Devin snatched her by the shoulders and twisted her around. Pinning her arms to her sides, he looked directly in her anguished face.

"I don't want to hurt you anymore. I'm not trying to hurt you. Royalty is my woman, and I love her. If she will have me, I want her to be my wife. Please...you have a man now, and I hope he's the one for you because I have never been the one. We have never been good for each other. Please leave and never come back. Please, Mel."

Her face crumpled and she wailed so loud, I could practically feel her heart-wrenching pain. Devin hugged her tightly, rubbing her back, calming her with his words of apology. Looking over her shoulder, his eyes begged me to understand that he owed her this one last act of compassion. After an interminable period passed, he pulled away and guided her gently to her car. She straightened up in the front seat and turned the key in the ignition. He watched her until she drove away.

Devin then pulled me out of the car and lifted me into his strong arms. I wrapped my legs around his waist. Kissing me wildly, possessively, he held on to me effortlessly before he slammed my car door and strode back into his home.

Pressing me up against the wall next to the front door, he untied the belt and opened my robe. His beard rubbed against my skin as he suckled my nipples long and hard, causing the muscles in my stomach to clench. I kissed him on his cheek, his eyes, his forehead, any of his sweet and salty skin I could touch with my lips, needing him inside of me desperately.

He lowered his sweats enough to free his stiff erection and entered me roughly, spreading my legs wide, pinning my thighs to the wall. He pounded me hard until our bodies shuddered in ecstatic release. Our mating, though animalistic and frenzied, affected me to the depth of my soul. Not only had he become my prince, he had become my king.

18

ROYALTY

I left Devin on Sunday more in love than before and determined I wouldn't let my fear interfere with him knowing the truth. He had been so honest and real with me. I had to trust his word that nothing would change between us once I finally became real with him.

On Monday morning, while eating a quick breakfast of Eggo waffles and juice, Ryder asked, "Mama, Blake wants me to hang out at his house on Saturday."

"I don't know Blake or his parents." I picked up my hickory brewed coffee from my Keurig and leaned on the counter, watching him eat at the kitchen table.

I'd always been hypervigilant when it came to Ryder spending time with other children and their families unless I knew them. He had some friends from his former school and the Boy Scouts, and I'd gotten to know their parents well. So far at Oak Ivy, I hadn't had the opportunity to meet any of the students or their parents.

"So? I'm in middle school now, and I can speak up for myself if an adult is trying to hurt me."

"Yes, you are more than capable to speak up for yourself. I still don't know who he is."

Ryder sighed loudly. "He's in my pre-algebra class and is on the baseball team. I have his number. I can just ask for his mother's number and you can talk to her. Come on, Mama, I want to go by his house. I'm not asking to spend the night. Just hang out with him on Saturday instead of Tee Rain. He has a pool and everything."

"Well Tee Rain also has a pool, and you're supposed to be with her and then join me for dinner to meet someone special. Saturday is not a good time."

"I don't really want to meet Mr. Anthony again."

"Anthony?" I'd called Anthony right after the weekend of the wedding to tell him that I'd just begun a relationship with another man. As I expected, he took it in stride and told me to take care. I'd forgotten about him until Ryder just mentioned his name.

"Yeah, the man you want me to meet...that guy at Tee Rain's dad garage."

Raini was right, my son was more perceptive than I gave him credit.

"It's not Mr. Anthony."

"Whoever it is, I'd rather hang with Blake and then I can go see Unc Tre and Tee Raini while you entertain *him*."

"Ry, the man I want you to meet is your father."

He frowned. "My father?"

I put my cup down and moved to sit next to him. "Yes, we've recently reconnected, and I would like you to meet him."

"I already told you I didn't care if we ever met."

"Well, he wants to meet you, and I think it's time for you to get to know him."

Ryder lifted his head, expression blank. "Can I go to Blake's house?"

I narrowed my eyes. "This is not a negotiation."

"The way I see it, you don't know Blake, and I don't know my father. I guess on Saturday we will both meet two people neither of us really want to meet." He stood up, leaving his half-eaten plate. "Mama, we need to go, I want to get to school early."

"Ryder..."

His eyes flashed. "Why would you tell me right before I go to school that a man I've never met wants to now?"

"I didn't mean to tell you until tonight. Give him a chance. I know you will like him and maybe one day even love him." I walked behind my son. Without looking at me, he placed his school's baseball cap on his head and his bookbag on his shoulder. "You always wanted to meet him."

"I used to when I was little, now I don't." He opened the front door and made it to the car before I could close it.

Once we were on the way to school, I said, "We can talk later if you want, but he's coming here on Saturday night."

"I guess I don't have a choice in anything." He folded his arms across his chest and stared out the passenger window.

"What's that supposed to mean?"

"Nothing."

"No, we are not passive aggressive. If there is something you need to say, say it."

"What difference does it make if you're not going to listen anyway."

"I always listen to you."

"No, you don't, Mama." His eyes flashed. "Everything is what you want. You want me to meet my sperm donor even if I don't want to. I don't even like this school, but you don't care. I have a chance to make a friend who's in my class, and because you've made plans for me, I can't go."

Not willing to accept that my son, who'd always been popular, now struggled socially, I argued, "You have friends."

"Not at Oak Ivy, Mama. There's not many black kids, and I'm the only one in my gifted class. The other kids have been at this school since kindergarten, and they don't care about making new friends. Every lunch, I'm in the library studying because I don't want to try to figure out who I should sit with at lunch. Geez, Mama, I only joined the baseball team to make friends."

Alarmed I said, "Ryder, I didn't know you were having such a rough time. Why didn't you tell me?"

"I tried, but every time you would give me a lecture or speech about the great education I'm receiving." He bowed his head. "You already got enough to worry about besides me and my lack of friends."

His dejection left me helpless, wishing I could do something that would make him feel better. I'd made my son believe that he didn't have a voice and that he had to carry his burdens alone. No, there *was* something I could do. Immediately, I pressed the button on my steering wheel and said aloud, "Call work."

When my paralegal answered, I smiled at Ryder. "Anne, I'm not coming in today. Tell Mr. Craig he'll have his report by tomorrow morning, and apologize for me for being tardy, but right now, I need to spend time with my son."

"No problem, Ms. James."

Ryder looked confused when I suddenly made a U-turn on a busy street. "We're both playing hooky today. Whatever you want to do today, the choice is yours."

"But I have a test."

I tapped his button nose. "So?"

His lips curved into a wide smile. "Why, Mama?"

"I want you to know that nothing is more important than you, and I don't care what's going on in my life, I always want to know the good and bad of yours. I need to spend a day with my favorite son in the whole wide world and we can figure out this friend thing."

He practically hopped in his seat in excitement. "In that case, neither one of us finished breakfast, and I could really use some pancakes and bacon. And then there's this video game I've been wanting you to buy."

"IHOP and then GameStop it is." I leaned over and kissed his soft, still chubby cheek, and he wiped it off playfully. "If you're not ready to meet your dad, I can let him know that you're not ready. I was wrong to tell you something so monumental and think you could go to school like normal. I'm sorry."

"You think he's going to like me?" Ryder asked hesitantly.

Stopping at the red light, I glanced at him. "He's going to love you like I do, and we can all talk and sort everything out. Any questions you have about him, I want the three of us to discuss together, okay?"

He tilted his head to the side and watched me with a sly smile. "Then I guess I can meet him after you pick me up from Blake's house."

Shaking my head, I responded wryly, "You already have your daddy's ways."

❦

"BABY, I WANT US TO TALK BEFORE RYDER GETS HOME. I asked Raini to pick him up from a friend's house. I want to tell you about him, show you some pics and even show you his room. Okay?"

"Sounds like a plan. Maybe we can get a quick fuck in. It's been days since I felt you."

I teased, "Damn, you get some of me and you can't get enough."

"I need to play *Insatiable* anytime I'm around you. That's why I'm anxious to meet Ryder so we can hurry the getting to know each other part and move on to spending time together as a family."

"You see us as a family even though you never met him?'

"Yes. I love him because he's a part of you."

Suddenly it never felt more urgent for him to know the truth. "Dev...baby, can you come now?"

"Now who's the one who can't get enough?"

"I'm being serious."

"I have a meeting in a few, but I'll be there as soon as it ends.

Royalty, I can hear the worry in your voice, but it's going to be okay. Even if he doesn't like me initially, he will. I have a way with kids, too. Got to go. Love you."

"I love you." I hung up my cell, praying that he was right and that we would all be okay.

19
DEVIN

"Tawnie, we have to be diligent on this case, or the bastard walks."

I pushed away my notepad and looked at my right-hand attorney who had been with me since I first opened the doors to my firm twelve years ago. We were meeting in my office about one of my clients who had been harassed by the police and were in the throes of a lawsuit with the NOPD. I had already won a civil case against them two years ago, and my client at the time had been awarded two million.

Tawnie flipped her bang and tapped her pen on my desk. "Devin, I know that. It's why I'm sitting here with you on a Saturday instead of under my girlfriend."

I cracked a smile. Tawnie was good at keeping my temper in check, especially when a case affected me. My cell beeped for the third time.

"Please answer it this time, you need a distraction. Ooh, I hope it's that sexy woman of yours."

I shook my head and warned, "She's strictly dickly."

"I can be persuasive."

I laughed and answered without looking at the caller ID. "Hello."

"Mr. D, can you come pick me up?" a child's trembling voice asked.

"Lil J?" Last week, I'd seen Lil J again during Career Day at his school. He had learned during my talk that my father was the former mayor, and Lil J wanted to know if I could arrange a meeting for the three of us. I'd given him my card and instructed him to have his mother call me.

"Yes. Please, can you come pick me up?"

"Where are you? What's going on?"

"I...got...arrested today. I didn't know anyone else to call. Too...scared to call...my mother... I think I need a lawyer." I could hear the fear behind his words.

"Shh...shh...I'll be right there, okay. Which precinct?"

Tawnie interrupted, "Devin, we have to get a handle on..."

Waving her to silence, I grabbed my bag and keys, still holding my phone, waiting for Lil J's response. I briefly muted the phone. "Tawnie, reschedule...it's an emergency. I'll call you later."

She popped up at the urgency in my voice. "Is it a new client? Do you need me to come with you?"

"No. I got this."

When I rushed into the precinct a few minutes later and saw Lil J sitting tall, trying unsuccessfully to hide his nervousness, handcuffed to the chair in front of one of the officer's desks, I thought my head would burst into flames. I strode to his side and bellowed, "Why in the hell is this child handcuffed?"

The police officer sitting at his desk jumped to attention. "Mr. Toussaint, we didn't know you knew him."

"Let him go now. What happened?"

The young white man stood up and explained, "This boy and his friends tried to break into a car."

Lil J looked up at me with red eyes. "Mr. D, I didn't do it. The—"

Another older white officer who still sat at his desk ordered, "Shut up."

It took all my will not to jack up this dumb fuck. I stalked over to him and leaned down in his face. "You say another fucking word to this child, and I'll have your job and your pension by the end of the day. Get those damn handcuffs off him. *Now.*"

The police tried to bluster, but the young officer wisely intervened and unlocked the handcuffs. Lil J stood awkwardly and rubbed his wrists. I instinctively opened my arms and folded him into my embrace. Tears ran down his face as he cried in my jacket.

I spoke in a quiet voice. "Shh...it's okay. I'm here now and no one, and I do mean no one, will hurt you."

The young officer began again. "Mr. Toussaint, he and his friends were caught trying to break into a car. The other three boys' parents came to pick them up already."

Lil J mumbled against my chest. "They weren't handcuffed."

"Excuse me?" I looked down into his hurt face. "Tell me again what you just said."

He gestured toward the younger cop. "He handcuffed me, but not the other boys."

The officer protested, "That's because he tried to resist arrest and one of the other boys said it was his idea."

"I didn't resist arrest. I swear to you, Mr. D, I didn't know what they were planning to do. I was visiting someone I thought was a friend. He and his friends wanted to walk around the neighborhood, and they thought it would be fun to see if we could break in a car. I immediately told them no and started walking back to the house to call my mama to pick me up because I left my phone. Someone must have called the police, and they picked me up as I walked back to the house.

"One of the other boys told the police it was my idea even though I wasn't near the car. When the cop asked me my name, I told him that I needed to have an adult with me before I answer any questions, and only if my parents or lawyer want me to respond. He then grabbed my wrist and handcuffed me. Once we got here, he handcuffed me to the chair, but the other boys sat next to me unchained."

"Were the other boys white?" I asked, though I knew the answer.

He nodded.

The older police officer began talking fast. "Look now, Mr. Toussaint, you may be a big-time lawyer and your dad the former mayor, but we have laws for a reason."

I asked tersely, "Where is Captain Bledsoe?"

The young officer responded, "In his office."

"I need him here, now. Tell him Devin Toussaint needs to speak to him." I placed my arm around Lil J's shoulder. "Let me handle this, and I'll take you home."

He nodded, giving me a relieved smile.

A few seconds later, the captain, an older heavy-set man with brown skin, walked out hurriedly, looking concerned. "Mr. Toussaint."

I pointed at the officers. "I want these sorry-ass cops who arrested this young man placed on immediate suspension without pay until they attend required training from the agency of my choice, or this precinct will face the biggest lawsuit for racial discrimination in this parish."

The captain frowned. "Without pay? You think that's necessary?"

"You don't want to know what I really want to do." I hit the desk, pissed. "They don't know the rage, the helplessness that we feel when we see our children, like this child, handcuffed to a chair in front of everyone to see. How it feels to be treated less than because of his fucking skin color." I moved closer to the offending officer, who took a step back. "You need to be fired, but all you would do is find a way to blame black people for your plight and continue to hate us instead of seeing that little boy as a fucking human being. And if I put my fucking hands on you, which is what my instincts tell me to do, all you would do is kill me and cover it up."

Captain Bledsoe raised his voice. "That's enough, Toussaint."

"You should have told these so-called officers that's enough!" I yelled. "For God's sake, you have the power to shut this racist cop shit down, fucking use it. They need to be trained to see their own bias. This ten-year-old child may be traumatized forever by being handcuffed to a chair surrounded by cops who have the potential to kill him in a heartbeat, with no consequences. You don't think he already knows what it means to be a black boy in the hands of racist cops? Meanwhile, you have sympathy for those white boys who you allowed to sit patiently waiting for their parents uncuffed.

"For them, this was a childish mistake they can look back on, maybe even with humor, but for *this* child, it became the scariest *life-threatening* situation he has ever been in." I looked around the now quiet precinct, all eyes on me. "No one in here saw anything wrong with this picture? No one suggested or tried to take the handcuffs off this child? Shame on every single officer who claims they're here to protect and serve but who really only offers that service to people who look nothing like me or this child."

I looked down at Lil J. "Wipe your eyes, son. This man did not have the right to question you without a parent or an attorney present. I'm not going to let you walk out of here with scars. Do you hear me?" He straightened his shoulders and nodded. I turned him around to face the police officer who handcuffed him. "Look at this innocent child that you must have perceived as a threat to cuff him. Yet, he's no different than anyone else's child in here, but instead of doing your job and discerning the obvious truth, you went for the stereotype. Now, apologize."

The offending officer's face reddened.

Surprisingly, the older officer stepped forward and lowered to Lil J's level. "I'm sorry for how we treated you."

Lil J nodded and the cop straightened and nudged his partner.

Captain Bledsoe ordered, "Apologize. Then I want to see the both of you in my office."

Lil J stared directly into the officer's eyes, shoulders up, head held high, no fear or sadness in his countenance anymore, waiting for his apology.

The officer averted his gaze and mumbled his apology.

I asked, "Did you mumble when you arrested him?"

He met Lil J's defiant glare and said, "Sorry."

I guided Lil J by the elbow toward the exit. "Captain, I'll send you my recommendations of diversity trainers Monday morning. And these two are not to return to duty until training is complete."

Captain looked annoyed at his men. "Okay, Mr. Toussaint. I'll be expecting your call."

As we headed out of the building, people clapped, and a few asked for my card on the way to the car. I nodded in acknowledgement, giving them cards as my rage dissipated, grateful that my power resulted in a positive outcome to Lil J's unfair arrest and treatment.

I unlocked the door for us and slid in the driver's side and waited until Lil J buckled up to talk.

"Why did you call me? I'm glad you did, but you should have called your mother first and had your mother contact me. The police were too scared to question my appearance in their precinct and assumed that I had permission to pick you up. The truth is, you shouldn't have been allowed to leave with me."

"I couldn't call my mother. She would be so hurt and disappointed. She's always lecturing me about how the world doesn't see me, and I need to be careful of the friends I choose. I knew I could trust you. Please don't tell my mother. I swear to you, I didn't know what they were up to. I walked away and still got in trouble. I finally thought I was making friends, but they lied to the police about me," he bit out angrily.

I sighed. "I believe you, but I still need to tell your mother. I would want to know if my son was arrested."

He looked down at his cell. "Okay. Can you please take me to this address?"

By the time we arrived at the warehouse district, Lil J was asleep. I checked the address again, and the building looked like an art studio. Maybe his mother lived in an apartment or condo on the second floor.

I shook Lil J's shoulder. He stretched and blinked several times as he woke up.

"Hey, is this the right place?" I asked.

"Yes, sir."

We got out the car, and the moment I saw the name on the door, Raini opened it. "Devin?"

I looked down at Lil J, confused. "Is this your son?"

Lil J answered, "No...this is my Tee Rain. I need her to tell my mother. Maybe she won't yell as loud if she tells her what happened?"

I watched Raini's face, and she looked worried. "Um...your mama doesn't know you're here?"

"No. I got into some trouble, and Mr. D came to help me. You should have seen him handle them cops. He told them off, made them apologize to me and everything!" His face beamed with pride.

Her eyes grew wide. "Cops? What happened? How do you know Ryder?"

My heart began to race. Ryder is not that common of a name. "Ryder? He told me call him 'Lil J.'"

Ryder added, "Yeah...for James. My real name is Ryder James." He shifted from foot to foot. "Tee Rain, I really have to use the restroom."

"Go ahead. I'll finish up with Mr. Devin."

Lil J—Ryder—looked back at me with...with my smile. "Are you going to still be here once I finish using the restroom?"

My God, he seemed familiar when I met him because he looked like I did as a child. No wonder Royalty had been vague about his age, waving me off when I asked. I should have suspected something...anything, but I was so caught up in winning her over, I'd been blinded to what had been so obvious.

"Umm...I need to go." Trying to control the shakiness in my voice, I reassured him, "Promise we'll spend time together soon."

"Thank you again for coming to get me." He hugged me tightly, and I held him to me, suddenly scared to let go, wondering if I was in a nightmare or a beautiful dream all at the same time.

I watched him run inside the studio. With the wind knocked out of me, I leaned into the wall next to the door for support. "Raini, and please don't lie to me...is Lil...Ryder my son?"

Eyes filled with worry and concern, she nodded. "Royalty is at home. Let her know I'll keep Ryder overnight."

20
DEVIN

I drove so fast to get to her, I don't know how I made it to her home alive, or how the police didn't pull me over for speeding.

Royalty opened her front door slowly, eyes already red and puffy.

"He's my son? My son?" I stared at her incredulously.

"I planned to tell you today. Had Raini keep him so you and I could discuss the best way to introduce you, but..." She opened the door wider.

"What the fuck is happening?" I closed my eyes, the world spinning for a second. I pushed past her and stormed into her living room. Pacing, I muttered, "I have a son."

Royalty watched me and asked cautiously, "How did you meet him? Why did he call you?"

"He's the boy that I started mentoring...or something." I stared at my balled fists, wondering once again if I was paying for my past actions. At what point would it end? "No matter what I do, I keep getting blindsided by women." I looked up at the ceiling. "God, how long do I have to pay for what I did? How long?"

"Devin, this is not about getting back at you or God's way of punishing you."

"Then why the fuck didn't you tell me that I have a son? How old is he?"

"He'll be eleven on his next birthday, in June," she said in a small voice.

Royalty's face blurred as I tried to make sense of words. I dropped onto her sofa. "My own flesh and blood has been in this world for a decade. I told you how much I wanted a child, how much regret I had that I couldn't make it work with my ex. Not because we were this great couple, but because we had a family. I loved that little girl with all my heart, and because she wasn't my biological, I had no rights. And all along, I had a son? A son I could have raised, whose life I could have been a part of? I could have given him what my father never gave me."

She eased down next to me. "You can still do those things. He's young, and he must already respect and admire you to call you before he called me." She rubbed her hands against her thighs. "We can get a paternity test if you prefer."

"You think I need a test to prove that boy, who I instantly had a connection to without knowing who he was, is my son? He has my skin color, my smile, and I can already tell he'll be as tall, if not taller, than me."

"I just wouldn't want you to think I'm trying to trick you or—"

I stood up, furious. "You avoided me for years, and after seeing me again, I had to pursue you. Why would you believe that I thought you tricked me? No, you didn't trust me enough to tell me the truth. No matter what I've said to you, trying to show you I changed, you still didn't trust me. You continued to date me for *two months*, and not once did you open your mouth to tell me about my own child. You pretended your child was some other man's child. Ten long years I will never get back. You've been lying to me all this time. I could have spent at least these last two months getting to know him instead of trying to win your heart. A heart I'm not sure I want anymore."

She jumped up, eyes wide with alarm. "I swear to you, I wanted to tell you so many times, but I was afraid. This shouldn't change us. We can be a family now."

I retorted, "We could have always been a family."

Royalty scowled. "Are you kidding me right now? The man who is in front of me now is not the man I met ten years ago. Back then you only cared about yourself. You didn't care about the woman you were married to when you were fucking me, and you damn sure didn't care about me beyond what was in between my legs."

"Why do you keep saying that? You meant the world to me back then. You never gave me a chance to show you I could be there for you and our child."

"The moment I realized that I was pregnant, I already knew two things—I was keeping the baby and that I loved you. You'd started calling and traveling more often to see me, so I stupidly thought that even if you had someone, it can't be anyone serious. That maybe you would be there for me and the baby. Except the day I found out I was pregnant, you texted with yet another change of plans, and my gut told me to finally do that search on you I'd been avoiding. I stumbled upon your wedding announcement. Your nuptials made the fucking society pages because a prominent Congressman's daughter was marrying one of the most eligible bachelors in New Orleans, the son of a state senator. You wouldn't have left her. You were and still are a public figure, Devin. You would've treated me like shit for bringing this scandal, this drama to your life."

"When have I ever treated you badly? Ever? You never once asked for more, never even hinted you wanted more—jokingly told me I would break your heart when you were the one who broke mine."

She pressed her fist against her heart. "Can you please wake the hell up and take some damn responsibility for your past actions and why I may have believed you wouldn't be there for me and our son?"

With the pain so excruciating that I needed a release, I roared louder than I could ever recall, "You never gave me the chance to live up to my responsibilities! Yes, I might have been scared, angry, and whatever fucking emotion you feel when something so life-changing and unexpected happens. But I would have gotten over it. Women talk about their fucking rights all the motherfucking time. What about my rights?" I slammed my palm against my chest. "I made that boy, and I don't get to be a part of his life because you decided that you didn't want to be hurt by me. Worried about your feelings, not concerned that your baby needs a father, or that I needed him. Or did it even cross your mind that I would want to know my son regardless of what happened between us? No, you didn't tell me because you were afraid of being rejected by me, not because you were afraid I would reject my child."

She backed an inch from me and sat back down. "Please calm down. You're scaring me."

"You think I would hit you?"

"No, baby. I know you wouldn't do that, but I can see your veins bulging out your neck and your forehead. You're going to give yourself a heart attack."

"And realizing that the boy I'd been spending time with is mine isn't enough for me to have a heart attack? Don't worry about me anymore." I ran my hands over my head. "What does he even think of me? That I'm a deadbeat, that I didn't want him, what?"

Royalty perched at the edge of the sofa, hugged herself, and began rocking. "I told him that you lived in another city and were too busy with your career and wasn't ready for a family. That it wasn't personal."

"And every time he asked about me, you repeated that to him? That I didn't want him."

"I never said you didn't want him."

"Doesn't matter what you said, I bet that's what he believes." Unshed tears threatened to fall. "That boy needed me his whole life. I know my absence affected him, made him feel less than, somehow. I grew up with my father and he made me feel less than because he had no time for me, never really wanted to know me. I can't imagine how Ryder must feel thinking his whole life that I didn't give a damn about him."

"I've been doing a good job without you. Ryder knows he's not less than. I raised him to believe in himself to be great. There are plenty of single women raising boys every fucking day and they grow up to be exemplary men."

I pointed at her. "There's a reason it takes a man and a woman to have a child, Royalty. He needed me, and you know it." She looked down at her hands, quiet. "What am I supposed to do with this information? How am I supposed to feel?"

"I don't know, but you have to forgive me. I didn't know what else to do."

"What about now? Huh? We've been seeing each other, loving each other, and you were still afraid to tell me that we have a child together? That night on the beach when I laid myself bare to you, why didn't you open your damn mouth and tell me then?"

Royalty reasoned, "That night you told me how angry you were about losing Nya and the threats you made to her mother. Nya wasn't even yours, but you were prepared to go against a man much more powerful than you just to keep a child that wasn't yours."

"Then you know and understand how I feel about children."

"All I could think was that you had the power to take him away from me, and I couldn't allow that. He's all I have. I'm not like you. You get to see your family every day if you choose."

I moved closer to where she still sat on the sofa, forcing her to bend her head back to look at me. "Then why keep seeing me at all? Huh? If you thought me capable of taking my son away from his mother, that I'm that much of a monster, why would you even want to be with me?"

She grabbed the bottom of my shirt. "Because no matter how hard I fought it, there is no other man for me. I had to be sure that your feelings for me were strong enough that you would never take him away."

I stared at the woman who'd now broken my heart twice. "'No matter how hard you fought it'? So, if I didn't feel the same for you or hurt you in some way, you wouldn't have introduced us? Wow." I strode toward the front entrance.

She blocked my path, spreading her arms across the door. "Devin, I didn't mean it like that. I've been pining for you since I texted you years ago that our relationship was over. The day I gave birth to your son without you by my side, and anytime anyone ever mentioned you or your father's name, my heart ached. The day at the market when I ran into you again, I could see and feel the desire you still had for me. I was surprised. I never expected you would still want me after all these years. I still loved you and couldn't believe that maybe I had misjudged you and that I'd made a terrible mistake not telling you about Ryder. And I didn't know what to do, so I ran from you."

"Well, now *I* don't know what to do." I moved around her, and she grabbed my arm.

"What about Ryder? Are you just walking away from him, too?"

Shaking my head vehemently, "No. I want a relationship with my son. I'm not sure I want one with you."

"Devin, you don't mean that...we love each other too much." She suddenly pulled my head down, kissing me, and when I tried to turn my head, grabbed my chin. Her other hand snaked down into my pants before I could stop her, and my betraying dick jumped to life at her familiar touch. She whispered against my lips, "Don't leave me, I need you...I need you. You promised nothing would change... Please."

Royalty backed me up to her sofa, coaxing me with her

tongue and her massaging hand. She shoved me down on the soft cushions, pushed her panties down her legs and mounted me. I spread my arms along the back of the sofa, letting her do the work of pleasing me. She quickly unzipped and freed me before she lifted her dress to slide down on my hard dick. She gripped my shoulders and I closed my eyes. Letting my head rest against the sofa, I enjoyed the feel of her slick, engorged walls as she rode me hard and fast with her warm and wet pussy, trying to make me forget that she hurt me, that she'd lied to me.

With every pump of her body on top of mine, I hoped for mind-numbing pleasure, hoped for a blissful oblivion, yet only anger remained. I couldn't ignore the blinding pain of betrayal. Resentment took hold of my emotions as I watched her in action, her eyes closed, mouth slightly gaped in sweet agony, the bounce of her braless breasts confined by material.

Needing her to feel my hurt, I tore open the front of her dress. My touch was admittedly cruel as I grabbed her breasts and squeezed, wanting her to know the pain coursing through my veins. Although she winced, she flung her head back, giving me free rein to her beautiful body. I took one of her stiff dark tips into my mouth and sucked hard and long while my hands relentlessly moved her hips against me. Her panting increased exponentially when I began fucking her. I could tell her end was near, but I wasn't ready for her to climax while I remained in misery.

I lifted us off the sofa. Her sugar walls refused to let go of the grip she had on my dick, and I knocked over the coffee table to place her on the rug so I could pound her mercilessly. I needed to purge all my negative emotions when I climaxed inside of her. I wanted to forgive and love again.

As I hovered over her, Royalty ripped open the buttons of my shirt to bite my nipple. While her pink manicured nails dragged scars on my back and my ass, I plunged deep within her. Her aggressiveness spurred me to fuck harder and faster, kicking over some other piece of furniture. We both desperately needed this physical release. She begged for a euphoric escape when I raised one of her legs high and found her G-spot and punished her tight, wet pussy again. I didn't stop thrusting until tears ran down her face. With a thunderous roar, my arms finally giving out, I fell on top of her.

21

ROYALTY

I heard voices at the door.
"Shit!" I screeched, and hit Devin's exposed chest through his torn shirt. He'd fallen asleep next to me on the floor. The room was a disaster. During the midst of our angry, guilty, passionate, crazy sex, we'd destroyed my living room.
"What?" He opened his eyes, rubbing his temples.
"It's Ryder. He can't see us like this."
Devin hurriedly zipped his pants before he started gathering the papers and décor that he'd knocked over when he turned over the coffee table. "Hey, one of your breasts is out."
I looked down and the top of my dress had been ripped. I adjusted it to cover my nakedness as much as I could, when I heard the door open. I spotted my panties near the walkway and hissed, "Get my panties."
He had been straightening the pillow but gave up on fixing his shirt since I'd torn most of the buttons. Devin practically dove to pick my panties up and placed them in his pocket as Ryder and a worried Raini entered the room. The moment would've have been hilarious if we weren't both deathly afraid that our son would guess that his parents were having sex.
"Mama, we kept calling you and you didn't answer." He then

noticed Devin. "Mr. D, what are you doing here?" Ryder looked at me, at my unkempt appearance and then the room and his face crumpled. "What happened to this room? How do you know my mother?"

I took a step toward him. "Ry, let me explain."

He looked at me, his brow deeply furrowed. "How do you know Mr. D? Mama, what's going on?"

I clasped my hands together and exhaled a shaky breath. "He's your father."

Incredulously Ryder stared at me and then turned his attention to Devin. He accused with a jabbing finger, "Were you trying to trick me, get to know me, to see if you would like me since I didn't know who you were? Or are you pretending to like me just to get back with my mama?"

Devin raised his hands. "Lil J...I mean Ryder. I didn't know I had a...you were my...son, until today. I swear."

He yelled, "Don't lie on my mama."

I moved to him, gingerly. "He's not lying. He didn't know. I never told him about you."

Tears flowed fast down his confused face. "What?"

"He just found out when he saw Raini. I was going to tell him today."

"My father never knew about me? So you're the liar? I hate the both of you!" Ryder screamed before he ran out of the room and out of the house.

Raini attempted to go after him, but Devin grabbed her wrist. "You'll never catch up with him." He took off out the front door, running as if his life depended on it.

I hurried to the door and watched as Devin chased after Ryder, who ran down the sidewalk. He caught up with him at the corner and Ryder punched Devin in the stomach. Before he could punch again, Devin grabbed him into a hug.

Raini pulled me back inside. "Royalty, Devin can handle him. You can't stand outside half-dressed."

"I fucked up so much. Now they both hate me," I wailed.

"They'll both be fine. It's just a shock." Raini placed an arm around me and led me to my bedroom. "First, we have to get you some more clothes before they come back."

I sat on the edge of the bed, rocking while Raini grabbed a T-shirt and pajama bottoms out of my drawer.

"I tried to stall him, but Ryder was insistent on coming home. He kept saying that he was supposed to meet his father tonight and didn't understand why you wouldn't answer the phone. With all he went through today, he needed you and started crying. He wondered if you knew and were disappointed in him and didn't want to speak to him."

"What did he go through, and how did Devin end up bringing him to you?" Raini had only told me that Devin dropped off Ryder. He had put two and two together and was on the way to see me.

"You and Devin didn't talk?" She grabbed my dress off the floor after I pulled it off.

"Not about what happened with Ryder. He was too pissed at me for not telling him Ryder is his son."

"Are you and Devin okay?"

"I don't know. He said he didn't want to be with me anymore."

"If he doesn't want to be with you anymore, then at what point did the sex happen? Even Ryder could tell what you had been doing."

I pulled the T-shirt over my head and tugged on my pajama bottoms, body sore and tingling from Devin's furious thrusting. "I was losing him, and I wanted him to pour all his anger and frustration inside of me. I needed him to feel me, to remind him of our unbelievable connection."

"And?"

"I don't know. You and Ryder woke us up before I had a chance to see if Devin saw the sex as a reminder of our connection or simply a release for his emotions."

When we heard the back door open, Raini and I both rushed

into the kitchen. Ryder walked in, followed by Devin. Heart threatening to burst at the sight of the two people I loved most in the world, together in the same space, I hurried over and hugged them both. Neither one hugged me back.

I stepped back and touched Ryder's face. "You're okay?'

He shrugged.

Devin grasped Ryder's shoulders reassuringly. "Let me get a shirt out of my car and we can sit down and talk." As he walked past me on the way to the front door, he said, "He's probably hungry. Order something."

"Okay," I answered weakly.

Raini went to Ryder and bent to see his downturned face. "Hey, call me if you need to talk or you need me to pick you up if you get too upset, okay?"

He lifted his head enough to nod.

She kissed the top of his thick hair. "Remember, whatever your mother did, she did because she loves you more than you could ever imagine." Raini looked at me. "Everything is going to be fine. Call me later."

She closed the back door quietly behind her and I wiped my sweaty palms on the bottom of my T-shirt. "How about I order some Chinese?"

Ryder remained silent as he walked past me to grab a bottle of water out of the fridge.

I followed behind him. "Please let me explain."

"Mr. D told me that we would all talk together." He then tossed over his shoulder, "Or should I call him Daddy?"

"Ry..."

He plopped down at the kitchen table, still refusing to look at me.

I eased down next to him. "Baby..."

"I don't want to talk to you."

Coming back into the kitchen wearing a white Nike T-shirt, Devin scolded, "I know you're mad with your mother. So am I, but you will respect her."

I expected Ryder to say something smart back, but he replied in a softer tone, "Yes, sir."

Devin chose to sit on the other side of Ryder instead of the closest seat, which was next to me. I tried not to read too much into his behavior.

"What are we eating?" he asked.

"Um...Ryder hasn't told me yet what he wants."

He looked at Ryder. "Meat lovers pizza and Cokes?"

Ryder nodded with a slight smile and Devin returned it.

So far so good, I thought to myself as I used an app on my phone to order pizza. "How did you two meet each other anyway?"

"I had a meeting with the principal at Oak Ivy Prep and Ryder opened the door for me. Impressed with his manners and our easy connection, I asked Dr. Bennett could we sit and talk more in the main office. He told me his name was 'Lil J.'"

I rolled my eyes. "A nickname I've never liked."

"It doesn't matter if I like it," Ryder answered smartly.

Before I could reprimand him for his tone, Devin gave me a stern look before he continued speaking. "I gave him my card, told him to use it anytime. We saw each other again when I returned to the school for Career Day over a week ago. I had planned to reach out to him and offer to be a mentor if it was okay with his mother, since he didn't have a father in his life."

He shook his head, his jaw tightening. "Turns out I'm the deadbeat dad."

"Devin, I already told you my reasons why I didn't tell you about your son. Today is about moving forward and for you to meet Ryder."

"Well that happened, so now what?" Ryder asked.

Devin responded, "I want to start spending time with you. Maybe on the weekends first and then during the week I can take you to school sometimes. We can get to know each other, and I can't wait to introduce you to my side of the family."

"Wait, so my grandfather is the former mayor of New

Orleans?" A slow smile spread across his handsome face, so much like Devin's.

He acknowledged wryly, "Even my own son is more fascinated with my father."

"This is crazy, isn't it, Mr. D?" Ryder frowned. "I'm sorry, what do I call you?"

Devin smiled warmly. "I hope one day soon, you feel comfortable enough to call me Dad or Daddy. Until then, Mr. D is fine with me. Don't want to rush you, and I'm not going anywhere."

I watched them interact and the flow of conversation between them seemed so natural, as if they'd always known each other. I thought that Devin would be the interloper, the outsider, but now it seemed it would be me. Neither one had been able to look me directly in the face since they returned, and if I decided to leave the table, I figured neither one would care.

"So, you're my mom's boyfriend, too?"

Devin responded, "We were trying to work things out, but right now my priority is you."

Stunned, I quickly moved my trembling hands underneath the table. My question had just been answered. He didn't want us, as a couple, anymore.

"If you and my mom break up, what happens to you and me?"

"It doesn't matter what happens between me and your mother. You can't ever get rid of me. You're my son, and that will never change. I've always wanted a child, and had I known about you I would have been in your life from the beginning." Devin met my hurt gaze with his own. "Don't worry about me and your mother. Our goal is to make sure that you're okay and that you continue to thrive."

"Yes. We just want to make sure you're okay," I added. "Today has been a lot. I still don't know how you ended up bringing Ryder to Raini's workshop."

Ryder quickly looked at Devin and he nodded. He was

already deferring to his father, something he only did to me before answering an adult's question.

Ryder began speaking. "Blake and two of his friends who go to another school decided to break into a car for fun. I didn't want to, and though I walked away, the police arrested me anyway when they arrested the other boys."

I grabbed Ryder's hand. "Arrested? Why didn't you call me?"

Devin intervened. "It's okay. He called me."

I bit out, "It's not okay." I looked at Ryder, shaking my head. "I knew I shouldn't have let you talk me into letting you spend time with a boy I don't know. Arrested at ten years old. Seriously, Ryder?"

Ryder protested, "Mama, I told you I was walking away."

"Then how did you get arrested, too?" I demanded.

"The other boys lied and said it was his idea." Devin reached for my free hand and pressed my palm to the table. "He's been through enough for the day. He called me, I handled it, no further harm will come out of this. Ryder has no intention of continuing a friendship with Blake."

"But—"

"I'll tell you everything later. I can tell you're upset, but right now he doesn't need to be reminded all over again of what happened today."

"If you were me, you'd be concerned about what happened today if he was..." My words faltered.

"If he was my child," he finished, his voice raised. "Well he is, and I was livid with his treatment before I even knew he was mine. Like I said, we will talk later." Devin removed his hand and then looked at Ryder. "Hey, I need to go, but I want to pick you up tomorrow, if you don't already have plans."

"You don't want to eat?" I asked.

"Yeah, Mr. D., eat with us," Ryder pleaded.

His jaw tightened as he slowly rose from his chair. "Maybe next time."

"Mr. D, can I come hang with you now?" Ryder asked, and

my heart shattered at the fear he clearly had that he wouldn't see Devin again.

Devin's face immediately lit up. "Of course. Anytime. If it's okay with your mother."

"You're my father, right? You can't just answer without asking her?"

Devin kneeled next to Ryder. "This will be an adjustment for us all. But from now on, me and your mom will always confer with each other before making any decisions that impact you. I want you to come home with me, but your mama has been through a lot, too. She may need you to be here tonight."

Wanting to do something right tonight, I insisted, "Ryder, you go be with your dad. I'll be fine."

For the first time since I dropped him off at Blake's this morning, he looked at me with a smile. "Thank you, Mama."

"Go pack your overnight bag. Clean underwear, a change of clothes, toiletries."

"I have extra toothbrushes and deodorant. Just bring a change of clothes and underwear," Devin said.

Once he ran off happily, I looked up at Devin who now leaned against the kitchen counter across from me. "Will you and I be okay?"

He shrugged.

"Devin, you wanted us to be a family and Ryder already adores you."

"Not from your effort." His eyes flashed. "That boy was handcuffed to a fucking chair while his so-called white 'friends' could wait uncuffed for their parents. They lied on him and instead of hearing him, you were already questioning his actions."

I blinked back tears. "My baby was handcuffed. Why didn't he call me?"

"He was scared of disappointing you, and then you started speaking to him at the table as if he was guilty."

"I still didn't know what happened, and he knows I've told

him about making good choices because trouble is so easy to get into but hard to get out of."

"He did make a good choice and still got arrested. Today with the police wouldn't have happened if I had been involved in his life."

"You don't know that."

He pointed at me. "I do know that. He wouldn't be seeking friendship in the wrong places if he'd been surer of himself."

"I did have reservations about him spending time with this boy, but it was our compromise because he was upset about meeting you."

"Why was he upset?"

I looked at him, dreading telling him the truth. "He didn't want to meet you."

"Why?"

"He was afraid you wouldn't like him."

Devin started to retort but then stopped himself and walked past me into the living room without another word. I heard him call almost impatiently. "Ryder? You ready?"

I folded my arms on the table and laid my throbbing head on top. The nice dinner I planned was ruined, the chicken in the sink completely thawed, ready for me to bake. My relationship with Devin was up in the air, my son already preferring his father to me. I wanted to scream that my nightmare was becoming a reality.

The doorbell rang.

Head still down, I announced, "You can take the pizza. I'll eat something here."

I heard footsteps and a moment later, Devin placed the pizza and a plastic bag of ice cold can drinks on my table. "You need to eat. I'll pick something up for me and him."

Ryder came back into the kitchen, his duffle bag on his arm, happiness emanating from him. "Are you ready, Mr. D?"

I lifted my head. This was what I'd always wanted, for my son to meet his father and that they both would react the way they did tonight. Devin was right, we couldn't focus on us when he needed to build a relationship with his son. I dried my tears with the back of my hand, opened the pizza box, and grabbed a slice.

"This is actually all of our favorite pizza in the whole wide world. Are you sure I can't entice both of you to eat a slice or two and have some ice-cold Cokes before you leave?" I took a bite, moaning my pleasure, exaggerating its deliciousness.

Ryder tried to grab a slice. I quickly closed the box on his hand, teasing, "Nope, this pizza is for people willing to sit and eat with me."

He looked at Devin, who stood quietly near the table with folded arms. "Come on, Mr. D. Let's eat a couple of slices and then you can buy me dessert on the way to your house."

Devin reluctantly smiled. "You already sound like me." He slid in the chair next to Ryder and we had our first dinner as a family together.

22

DEVIN

I pulled up into the circular driveway of my family's home behind Nicholas's silver convertible Porsche, gearing up to speak to my father about Ryder. My mother would be happy and supportive. I had no idea how my father would react.

He loved Nya and had been the first to suggest I find any type of dirt on Nya's father to disparage his character, anything to show Nya's life was better with me. It had been the first time I realized how much he loved the little girl he believed to be his grandchild. Ryder is legitimately his blood and has the intelligence, looks, and charm of the men in our family. I wanted him to accept my son more than he'd ever accepted me.

On Sundays, my parents could always be found at home, the only routine and tradition my father maintained. He didn't go anywhere except to church and the occasional restaurant, but always with my mother. Sundays had been the only day I expected peace in my household because Derrick Toussaint actually tried to be a respectable father and husband.

I used my key to enter the home I grew up in, long since remodeled after Hurricane Katrina hit and the first floor had been flooded. We had been more fortunate than most that we only lost furniture and had the necessary insurance and means to rebuild. I lived in a condo downtown at the time, so I didn't lose anything. My mother had two large portraits of us as a family in the great room that I passed on my way to the deck—one when I was six and another when I was fifteen. The second picture included Nicholas because he had just started living with us.

I heard voices the closer I drew to the back of the sprawling house. My Aunt Darling, dressed in shorts and a T-shirt too tight and short for her advancing age, had just walked through the French doors when she noticed me.

I hugged my only aunt and Nicholas's wayward mother. "Hey, Tee."

She squeezed me tight before pulling back to look at me. "Devin, I didn't know you were stopping by today. I wouldn't have made plans elsewhere. I stopped by to speak with your daddy."

She only visited to ask for money, which always bothered my mother and Nicholas. I had my own problems with my family and didn't need to add my aunt's entitlement and my father's inability to deny her anything to my list.

"You knew Nicholas was going to be here," I reminded her.

She waved her hand and commented without any jealously or envy. "He only cares about his uncle and aunt. What are you doing here?"

"I have to tell the family some news. Can you stay?" I only asked out of politeness since I knew she seldom changed her plans for anyone, except for her latest fling.

Aunt Darling quickly kissed my cheek. "Just catch me up later, I have to go. Relax. Don't let my brother get to you. I keep telling you, he's all bark."

I nodded, watching her naturally long ponytail swish toward the front of the house before I continued on my way. When I stepped through the French doors and back into the humidity, fog filled my Versace sunglasses.

My parents and Nicholas were sitting around the umbrella-covered table by the pool eating boiled crabs, shrimp, crawfish, and spicy potatoes. They all looked up in surprise as I stepped onto the lawn. I pulled off my shades and wiped them.

Nicholas smiled. "Why didn't you tell me you were stopping by?"

"Do I need an invite to see my family?"

Ma beckoned me to the table. "My boy never needs an invite."

I kissed her cheek. "I just saw Tee."

My father said, "You only stop by when you need something, too."

"Act like you care and I'll stop by more."

He waved his hand dismissively. "It wouldn't kill you to stop by once a week, like Nick does."

Nicholas looked up at me apologetically. He understood my issues with my dad, and I forgave him for never addressing the obvious difference my father made between us.

I chose a seat in between my mother and Nicholas and grabbed one of the cold beers on the table. I took a long gulp before I announced, "I'll be visiting more because I have a ten-year-old son, soon to be eleven, and I want him to be a part of this family. I didn't know about him until two weeks ago, and I want you to meet him next weekend when he visits me."

None of them said a word.

Uncomfortable with my family's shocked silence, I rambled nervously, "I understand your reaction...mine was much worse. Crazy that I tried unsuccessfully to have a child, and the whole time I had one living less than thirty minutes away. But it doesn't matter because he's in my life now, and I'm already crazy about him. He's a charmer, wicked smart, looks like me...well, he looks like me and Royalty, his mother."

Finally breaking the quiet, my mother clapped her hands in delight. "I have a grandson? I'd almost given up on being a grandmother again."

"Do you know it's your child this time?" my father asked

drily. "I don't want to waste time getting to know one of 'your' children."

Fighting the overwhelming urge to get up and leave, I instead retorted, "I told you I knew Nya wasn't mine from the beginning but accepted her as my own to make up for what I'd put Nia through. Just like I was certain she wasn't my daughter, I'm certain Ryder is my son. Because you were hurt about Nya, I can forgive what you just said, but if you want a relationship with your only grandson, then all these hurtful and snide comments you say to me have to end."

My father continued as if I hadn't said a word. "Let me guess, you had this child while you were married?"

Without any guilt or shame, I responded, "Yes."

Nicholas asked, "Is that why Royalty had been avoiding you?"

"Yes."

Nicholas sat back in his chair. "Wow. I didn't expect that to be the reason." He tilted his beer toward me. "Congratulations. Can't wait to meet him."

I looked at my cousin, who had become my brother and best friend over the years. "Sorry I didn't tell you as soon as I found out."

Nicholas grinned. "Trust me, cuz, we have some talking to do."

Shaking his head, my father grumbled, "Bringing scandal on the family once again. It's not enough your wife publicly leaves you for a damn singer while I'm up for re-election, an election I lost, by the way. Now you're going to be all around the city with this boy who you obviously created while you were married. Have I taught you nothing?"

"You taught me everything I know, old man." I stood up, unwilling to compromise anymore with my father. "I don't care what anyone thinks or says about my life. If you don't want to have anything to do with your grandson, so be it. I'm stupid for even wanting to subject him to you and your concept of family anyway."

He scowled. "Says the man who doesn't know how to keep his wife."

"You've gone too far, Uncle Derrick!" Nicholas slammed down his beer bottle.

Suddenly, my mother slapped my father hard across his face, the unexpected sight and loud sound forcing me to jump back. My father grabbed his cheek and stared at his wife with stunned indignation.

"Shut up, Derrick! Shut up now. You over there acting holier than thou like you're honorable and above reproach because you and I are still married. When the whole city knows that I just never left your sorry ass." Ma then looked at me. "Nia was smart to leave you for a man she loves, and hopefully he's treating her better than you did. Sorry, son, but it's true. She deserved better. I hope you treat Royalty or the next woman with the respect you want women to give to you. Definitely better than your father ever behaved with me."

Nicholas and I remained silent, stupefied that my mother was finally speaking up.

She turned back to my father who still palmed his cheek, his mouth gaped open. "And if you do anything that will make Devin keep my grandson away from me, I swear it will be the last thing you do. I've put up with your women and your shit because I have been stupidly in love with you, and I stayed because I believe in family. All I did was contribute to how these boys treat women and the madness we call the Toussaint family. The shit, the craziness, the lies end today, and if you think I'm bluffing or I'll go back on my word like I have for years when it came to your infidelity, try me. Now, I need you to leave us so my son and I can talk about my new grandbaby." She patted the table for me to sit.

My father continued to rub his face, apparently scared speechless. I don't believe my mother has ever hit my father before, or addressed him like she just did.

Nicholas said, "Um, Auntie Chris, we're men."

"What?" She looked at him, confused.

"You said we were boys, but Dev and I are men." He cracked a smile.

"You start acting like men and then I'll call you that," she snapped back.

Nicholas laughed. "Well, I better start acting right."

I asked, "I'm already half-way there, right, Ma?"

She folded her arms. "We'll see."

Nicholas looked at my father, who remained silent. "Unc, I think Auntie told you to leave now."

"Yes, you heard her. Leave." I smiled as I plopped back down in the chair and kissed her cheek. "Proud of you, Ma. And I plan to do better by any woman in my life, the way I want my father or any *other* man worthy of you to treat you."

We hugged each other tight, and when she pulled back, Ma asked, "When can I meet my grandson? Oh, I'm so glad Royalty is his mother. You make a beautiful couple. I really like her for you."

"I know, Ma. But right now, we're both focused on being parents. If you want, I can pick him up tomorrow since it's Memorial Day, and we can have lunch at my house." I pulled out my cell, all of us ignoring my father, who finally rose from his chair. "I have some pics of him."

Ma happily grabbed my cell and her eyes teared. "Oh Devin, he's beautiful."

I beamed with pride. "Ma, you don't call boys beautiful."

My father took the cell out of his wife's hand. I gritted my teeth, waiting for the worst. He looked at the pic and his hand trembled as he spoke softly, almost reverently. "No, he is beautiful. He looks like you when you were that age." He then passed the phone back to my mother. As he headed inside the house, he said over his shoulder, "We'll both be there to meet our grandson, tomorrow."

My mother and I looked at each other and smiled.

Nicholas reached for another crab. "He's about to be so spoiled."

"He already is. I've already brought him so much junk, it's crazy."

Ma said, "So, tell us about my new grandson."

I settled in my chair, grabbed a few shrimp and cocktail sauce, and began bragging about Ryder to my family.

※

LATER THAT EVENING, BACK AT HOME, I PICKED UP MY CELL and dialed her number. I didn't know if she would answer since I'd hadn't spoken to her in over two years.

"Hello?" I could hear the surprise in her voice, and I sighed deeply at hearing the familiar, pleasant sound. Nia Winston Saint. She had been my wife for nine years, and I had only been a husband to her for two of them.

"Nia, it's me," I said.

She laughed. "I know it's you. I have your number, remember?"

"Guess I'm surprised you answered."

"You haven't called me in a long time. Had to make sure everything is okay. Is everything okay?"

"Yes. It is. I saw your dad and Ms. Shelly at Tre's wedding."

"Shelly told me since he's still not speaking to me."

Her father still preferred me to her new husband. I didn't realize that he'd stopped talking to his only child because of it. "I didn't know."

"I thought maybe you did since you still have your monthly lunches."

"We rarely talk about you, and I don't mean it in a negative way. I just assumed your father didn't mention you out of respect for me. He's going to come around because he does love you."

"Deep down I know that, but my dad is more stubborn than you."

Trying to lighten the mood, I joked, "That's a whole lot of stubborn."

"If you're calling me about Mel, Shelly said she saw Mel—"

"That's been over for two years."

"I really don't care when you two broke up, though I had already figured as much. Before you rudely interrupted me, I was going to say that Shelly saw Mel and said that she left upset after you kissed the maid of honor in front of everyone. Shelly said it looked like you and this woman were in love. Hope she's someone special."

"She is." I fought the wave of sadness at her mention of Royalty and the magical night we shared. "How is Nya?"

"Growing every day, giving me a run for my money with her abundance of energy."

I smiled. Only a dull ache remained hearing about Nya. "She grew so fast. We used to joke that she would run before she learned to walk, and we were right."

"We were right." There was a pause before she asked the inevitable question, "Why did you call after all this time?"

"I wanted you to hear from me before you heard from someone else."

"What?"

"I have a son, and he's the best thing that ever happened to me."

I could hear the smile in her voice. "Congratulations. I am genuinely happy for you. How old is he?"

"Thank you." I slowly tapped my desk with my pencil. "I just found out about him, and he's almost eleven years old."

"Eleven?"

"Yeah."

Her sigh was long and exhausted. "One more reason why I'm glad I left you."

I quickly added, "Look, I'm not trying to dredge up old hurts and resentments. I didn't want you to find out about another story without hearing the truth from me. I met someone early in our marriage and fell in love...the maid of honor Ms. Shelly saw me with at Tre's wedding, to be exact. She found out she was pregnant the same day she found out about you. She cut me out of her life without an explanation and never told me about my son until recently."

"Why are you telling me all of this? You don't owe me."

"I do. I owe you a lifetime of apologies."

"You apologized to me the day the divorce was final, and I've forgiven you."

"I know, but I always tried to justify my behavior, and there is and never was any reason for me to ever treat you the way that I did. I wanted you to know that if you ever thought you could have been or done something different, you shouldn't. You were always a good wife to me. You are a good woman, Nia, who deserved better than me, and I hope you've found that. I really mean that. Justin is a lucky man."

"Trust, my honey bear knows that. And I am an incredibly lucky woman."

"'Honey bear' for a grown man? He must *love* that."

"He allows it to humor me."

"Tell him it's better than your term of endearment for me."

"What did I call you?"

"Asshole," I teased. "You don't remember?"

She giggled. "You always could make me laugh."

"Hate that I ever made you cry."

"Me, too. But hey, everything happens for a reason. I would have never met Justin if not for Mel. And I never would have left you if you'd done right by me. So, I'm good, and it sounds like you are, too. I know how much you wanted to be a father."

"I love it."

"You still want me to send pics of Nya?"

"As often as you can. I will always love her."

"I can do that. Tell my dad I said 'hello' when you have lunch with him."

"I'll do you one better. I'll stop this madness and make sure he calls you while we're together."

"If anyone can make him do anything, it's you."

"Then it's done. Take care, Nia."

"Bye, Devin."

23
ROYALTY

I peeked around the curtain every night that Devin dropped off Ryder. We'd arranged for me to drop him off at summer camp as I'd always done. He picked him up, they ate dinner together, and then Devin dropped him home.

Devin refused to leave the car, and when I opened the door to receive Ryder, he waved politely, as if we were divorced parents instead of the passionate, loving couple we were becoming before he found out the truth. We only communicated by text and rarely spoke by phone, and only to discuss logistics about Ryder. His support was wonderful, and I finally had more time to focus on my work without guilt, and yet all I longed to do was be with him and Ryder.

That night we ate pizza together, we'd behaved like a family, both of us laughing at Ry, who had the gift of gab, as he talked about any and everything. I'd hoped that Devin would reconsider us being a couple after we'd enjoyed the meal, but his focus remained solely on developing a relationship with Ryder. I didn't know if he had truly given up on us or if he just needed more time with our son.

"Penny for your thoughts." Tresa smiled and bent to hug me before settling across the table from me.

I'd asked her to lunch because I needed talk to someone other than Raini ,who seemed to be on Devin's side these days and urged me to give him more time and space. Tresa appeared summer ready with her sun-kissed light skin, long blonde cornrows, and thin-strapped sundress.

"It's been a lot lately."

"I heard about you and Devin and Ryder." She picked up her menu. "It's been the talk of the city, especially because you two made quite the splash at my brother's wedding."

"What are people saying?" I asked with dread, not sure I wanted to hear the gossip people had been sharing about me.

"They think that you were Devin's mistress and that he had an outside family his whole marriage. And that Nia found out, which is why they divorced, and she took off with Devin's daughter and married Justin out of spite."

The waitress walked up at that moment and I ordered. "Two hurricane daiquiris please."

Tresa touched my wrist. "I don't really want any alcohol."

"They're both for me."

She raised her eyebrows before addressing the waitress. "This appears to be a drinking moment, so one of those will be for me, and bring us one of your seafood beignets to start." She looked at me. "You need to eat something if you plan to drink."

"I don't care if I get drunk. No one is home. Ryder is with his father again."

"Based on the tone you're using, Devin must be giving you the blues?"

"Not the way you think. He doesn't want anything to do with me outside of Ryder. He's still pissed at me for withholding the truth from him, but I did it because I didn't think he would accept his love child because of his prominence in the city. And yet we're still being judged like we'd carried on a torrid affair for eleven years."

"It's more because of his reputation than yours. The gossips are trying to figure out who you are."

"They can keep guessing. I just want my man back."

"Then get your man."

"It's been weeks, and he still won't talk to me. Everything is communicated through text and only to finalize plans for Ryder. I thought we could at least celebrate Ry's birthday together, but he texted to say that his family had planned a dinner for his birthday, and he would pick him up, not us, just him. He even opened a checking account and deposits money directly into it that only Ryder can access. Of course, he sent me a text stating that if I wanted him to pay back child support, he didn't mind drawing up documents. Ugh. I hate that everything between us is so technical."

"You did keep his son away from him. Were you ever planning on telling him?"

"I've always wanted to, especially when I found out about his divorce, but then I worried that he would take him away from me. I'd avoided social media for years to prevent Devin doing a search and seeing me and Ryder."

Tresa leaned forward. "Apparently you were meant to see him when you did, and you're supposed to be together. I've known Devin a long time, and I personally have never seen him so caught up. All those beautiful women at the reception vying for his attention, and he made it clear in front of everyone that you were the only woman who mattered. That whole make-out session when he put that garter on you made me blush, and I don't blush easily. Let go of your own guilt and fear and make that man listen to you. Yes, Devin can be stubborn and an arrogant asshole, but you know he's still crazy about you."

The waitress placed our drinks and appetizer in front of us.

Mulling her words, I picked up my drink. "You are absolutely fucking right. He does still love me, he's just hurt. Glad I decided to have lunch with you."

Tresa cut a piece of the cheese, crab, shrimp, and crawfish pastry and placed it on the little plate before pushing it in front of me. "Eat this first. I can tell you're losing weight."

I put my drink down and took a bite of the tasty morsel, my appetite coming back. "I also recall you and Nicholas had your own thing going on at the wedding."

"Girl, please, that 'thing' is over. We slept together that night and he's been running scared ever since. I don't have time to chase after no man." She ignored the straw and took a long gulp of her alcohol.

"Wait, don't tell me he wasn't good in bed?"

"Please, his kiss made me come. I'm still kicking myself for admitting I had deep feelings the next day. I know the type of man he is. Hell, I'm that type of woman."

"Tresa, I have eyes, too, and he was positively smitten with you that night. Maybe you caught him off guard because he didn't expect you to talk about your feelings."

"Oh, he told me first, and you're right, he didn't expect me to reciprocate."

"Then I'm confused."

"For people like Nicholas who loves the hunt, I made it too easy for him. He thought he would have to pursue me longer, and I'm almost certain that he didn't mean to tell me how he really feels." She took another swig of her drink. "I made love too real and appealing for a man who is either scared or doesn't want a relationship."

"So that's it? You have deep feelings for each other and have no intentions on acting on them?"

"I don't care about him anymore, and I don't chase after men, not even Nicholas Toussaint."

"I hear you." I pushed my untouched daiquiri in front of her. "You may need this more than I do, to help you pretend a little longer that you don't care, because I personally know the lasting effect of the Toussaint men."

Unable to disagree with me, Tresa proudly picked up the second glass and took another long gulp. "I think you and I are about to be best of friends."

24
DEVIN

"Um...Devin...the mayor is here to see you," Tawnie announced.

I straightened in my chair, wondering why Tre wanted to see me. He hadn't responded to my apology that I included in my letter to Raini, which I really hadn't expected. He had been politely distant towards me at his wedding and we spoke briefly when I, Ryder, and my parents attended his parents' annual Fourth of July barbecue.

"Send him in."

His huge bodyguard and friend, Taz, opened my door did a quick perusal of my office before he stepped back outside to let Tre enter. Tre walked in and closed the door firmly behind him. I stood to greet him. He extended his hand, and I grasped it slowly, still unsure of his visit.

"Excuse me for just dropping by, but I had a break in my schedule. We're both busy men. What I have to say won't take long."

"Sure." I gestured toward the leather chair in front of my desk and Tre unbuttoned the bottom of his suit and we both sat down. His expression and disposition were surprisingly pleasant as he looked around my office.

"What up?" I asked casually, as if we'd never stopped speaking.

Tre answered without skipping a beat, "Nothing but the sky."

I grinned, relaxing back in my chair. "Didn't think you remembered."

He shrugged. "We said it to each other every time we hung out."

Tre slightly frowned when he noticed the portrait on the wall behind me. I'd bought the painting from Raini the day I ran into Royalty again.

"I guess I should thank you for helping Raini get a showing in the warehouse district. I tried but she wouldn't let me."

"No thanks needed. I figured you'd made the offer to help long before me. Sometimes it's easier to receive help from someone who doesn't mean as much." I shrugged. "Besides, I owed her father."

"Can't believe you knew Raini's father."

"Crazy, small world, right? Deaux was one of the best men I've ever met in my life. He was there for me when I needed it the most. Didn't treat me like I had a silver spoon in my mouth, accepted me even though we were from different sides of town."

Tre looked pensive. "Wish I'd met him, especially because I had the chance to meet him once, and I punked out," he said, referring to when he and Raini were teens.

"Man, he was a big intimidating dude, and you were trying to holler at his precious daughter. I would have been the biggest punk, too. Deaux's size alone made him scary."

He nodded. "Then he was tatted all on his neck before it became popular."

"Yeah, he really turned his life around and still had street cred. Nobody could touch Deaux. You're doing a good thing with his shop. Help knuckleheads like I used to be but who don't have the resources we do." I paused a beat. "Remember when we used to party all night and during the day strategize, like we're sitting now, on how to elect me as District Attorney and you as mayor? Man, we thought we were on top of the world—young, black, professional, and successful. Obama was running for President, our fathers were lawmakers, we were following in their footsteps. Anything was possible. The sky was the limit."

The corner of Tre's lip curved. "Yeah. We were living proof of what the right education and background could and would do for black men."

"Does Raini know how wild you used to be? Remember stripping in front of those women at the club just because they dared you?" I laughed at the memory.

"No, she doesn't." Tre ducked his head. "Dev, it was Mardi Gras and I'd just turned twenty-one."

"Oh, okay. What about TJ's bachelor party when *you* gave the *stripper* a lap dance?"

His smile widened. "Alright, alright. My hot boy ways been over."

"We had fun back then."

Tre smiled. "We did."

Regret that I'd lost his friendship and loyalty hit me hard. "And I fucked it up because of a woman, a good woman, that neither of us ended up with anyway."

Tre sighed and rubbed his thigh. "We could've gotten past us liking the same woman. I thought we were boys. I just didn't understand why you couldn't tell me you liked her."

"I was too damn selfish and a coward back then."

"Don't forget jealous. It's the reason you were hitting on Raini once you knew she was mine."

I bristled at the truth in his words. I had been jealous of Tre even when we were friends. People were naturally drawn to his energy. He was meant to be a leader. "I was attracted before I knew she was yours. The alpha in me wanted to see if I had any effect once I knew she was your woman."

Tre grinned smugly. "Which you didn't."

I chuckled. "No, I didn't. I was meant to meet Raini so I could be..." My voice faltered, and I straightened my shoulders.

"So, you could be with Royalty," Tre finished and leaned forward. "Neither my wife nor Royalty know I'm here. I'm giving you this advice from one old friend to another. You were meant to see Royalty again when you did. Both of you are older, more mature, and available. I saw you at my wedding with her, and even I could see that you love that woman. More importantly, you have a son together. Don't waste any more time than you already have, and be that family you've always wanted. Let that damn foolish pride go, Devin."

I hit the top of my desk as anger and hurt rose within me again. "She kept him from me. Maybe she would have kept Ryder from me forever if I didn't bump into her again. You've known about your daughter since the beginning. Imagine how you would feel if you never found out about Tracie until she was ten years old. Your own flesh and blood is out there in the world thinking you don't give a fuck. Ryder told me that, and it broke my heart. I know how it feels to believe your father doesn't want you. It fucks with you."

"No, I can't and don't want to imagine my life without Tracie. She is my everything." Tre tapped his heart with two fingers. "But our circumstances in how our children came into the world were different."

"I know that, but I can't shake that every day Ryder and I spend together, I see how he was affected by my absence. He told me how he wanted to join the baseball team, not only to make friends but because he admired the coach since his grandfather and uncle live miles away. He also shared how much you have meant to him these past few months. Like me, Ryder had been searching for a father figure, needing guidance that he could only get from a man."

Tre protested, "Royalty is a good mother, and she has been raising Ryder right."

"She is a hell of a mother. It doesn't change the fact that children need their mothers *and* fathers. I've made some fucked-up decisions and treated women horribly because of my father who

I grew up with. Imagine if I didn't have him, I would be a worse man."

"Or a better man. Excuse my French, but Mr. Toussaint was a fucked-up example of a father." Tre held his hand up, anticipating my protest. "Don't forget I knew him even before I ran against him." He shook his head. "I've been a single father co-parenting with a woman whose values I still question, and I still believed my daughter would've been fine. Just like Ryder. Now he will just be a better man with you and Royalty in his life."

"You don't understand. I don't know if I can get past not seeing his first step, the first time he said 'dada,' teaching him how to stand up and pee. I missed out on so much because Royalty decided to be a single mother. I didn't make her one."

Tre clasped his hands together. "I do understand this. If Ryder disappointed you in any way, you would still love him."

I nodded emphatically. "My love for him will never be conditional."

"Then why can't you love Royalty the same way?"

"Come on Tre, you know as well as I do that love between a man and woman is different than between a parent and child."

"It shouldn't be different. Love is love, if you're with the right person, and Royalty is that person for you," Tre argued. "You want everyone to forgive you for the shit you pulled but you can't forgive the woman you say you love, for not trusting you enough with the truth during a time when you were newly married to someone else." Tre shook his head. "Have you even said it aloud to yourself? You were *married* to Nia, the fucking New Orleans princess, when Royalty was pregnant with your child. Real talk, like you love to say, we both have been guilty of being too focused on our images. As much as you would like to believe you would have accepted Royalty's pregnancy at that time, I can't say I believe you."

"Royalty never gave me a chance to decide if I wanted to be a father or not."

"Devin, Royalty didn't know you had a wife until she was

pregnant, and you expected her to believe that you would be there for her and Ryder?"

"Please say that again, Mr. Mayor."

I looked past Tre to Royalty, standing in the doorway, her black wavy hair flowing past her shoulders, wearing my favorite little black dress that caressed her curves perfectly. My queen looked so damn beautiful and fierce. My indignation immediately lifted, replaced with pure joy at the unexpected sight of the woman who made me believe that true love was possible.

"I need my king." She placed both hands on her hips. "This not talking to me has gone on long enough. I've been giving you space and time to know Ryder. I need you, too. And two months is long enough to go without you. Either you're going to be the man you told me you are, or continue being the selfish bastard you were."

Tre hopped up. "On that note, I better go. Don't want to be around for this conversation."

Dragging my happy eyes away from Royalty, I looked at Tre. "For whatever it's worth, or if it matters, no bullshit, I voted for you. You've always been the best candidate for mayor."

Tre's smile vanished and he blinked rapidly before turning around and tossing over his shoulder. "It matters." Tre kissed Royalty on her cheek and closed the door behind him.

Royalty strode to my desk. "Stop punishing me, Devin.

I eased back in my chair, her presence calming me. I missed her terribly. "Being without you is torture for me."

She visibly relaxed and demanded, "Then why are you doing this?"

"I didn't know how to feel about you, how to be around you anymore," I explained. "I've been wanting my own child for years, unfairly gave Nia hell for not giving me a child. Even claimed her child from another man as my own and became a better husband to her because I wanted someone to call me daddy. And I had a son all this time. A bright, handsome son who is the best of both of us, who you kept from me. A son who

I may have never known unless he came looking for me when he became a grown man. I believe he would have because he missed and needed me in his life. Did you know that?"

She admitted quietly, "I don't doubt it. He's always been better with men. He never really was a mama's boy. He loved when my brother or daddy would visit. He never told me how much he wanted to meet you, but that's probably because he didn't want me to worry or feel bad."

I pressed my palm against my heart. "I loved you back then, would have probably ended my marriage to be with you and my baby if you had told me."

Frustrated, Royalty said, "Devin, you don't know that. You were into your image, and truth be told, so was I. I didn't want to be the side piece of the mayor's son, hidden somewhere with your baby who you would sneak away to visit."

"I do know how strong I felt for you. How much I loved you back then. I thought you didn't feel the same, and since I was married anyway, I let you go. You have this whole scenario in your head that would've never happened."

"Even if we had married, we would be divorced. You know how you were with these women."

I shook my head vehemently. "I was a horrible husband to Nia because she wasn't you. No other woman can hold a candle to you, and if you'd given me a chance back then, we would have stayed together happily until death do us part."

"We can't change the past, remember? What we can change is now and our future." Royalty moved around my desk and pushed my rolling chair back to stand between my legs. She placed her hands on my thighs and licked my lips before giving me her tongue briefly. "You asked me to tame you, make you a better man. We have a son to raise together. I'm here now, and I'm not leaving this office until either we talk or sex it out. I prefer fucking."

"Thinking I want to fuck here." I slowly pushed the soft fabric of her dress higher until it was over her hips, revealing red lace panties. I slid the lace over so I could kiss her mound, and she affectionately rubbed the back of my head. "And talk more at our home."

"Our home?" She turned around and bent over.

"Shit." My dick grew impossibly harder at the sight of her naked plump ass, and I traced the tiny strip of material that ran between her cheeks. Standing and unbuttoning and unzipping my pants, I said, "Yeah, we'll have to put your house on the market, or we can keep it as rental property. I can arrange packers and movers to bring the stuff you want to my home."

She tried to turn around and I stopped her by firmly pressing her down on my desk until she arched her back. "Devin, you already making decisions without discussing them with me."

I entered her smoothly, closing my eyes in sweet, sweet ecstasy, my dick thanking me for choosing this pussy. After a few long strokes, I said, "Queen, did you even notice that I said I want you to live with me?"

"Yes," she moaned.

With every deep thrust, I punctuated my words. "And your answer will be yes, right?"

She smacked my desk hard and panted, "Is this how it will always be? Using your body to get me to submit to your will?"

I pumped harder. "I can't help that I have the power of persuasion in and out of the bedroom."

Royalty tossed her hair over one shoulder and arched her back even more, her slick feminine walls tightening around my pulsing member, eliciting a couple curse words from me.

"Don't forget I have my own powers that I plan to use too. Like you're coming with us to Okinawa next month to visit my parents."

Still rhythmically moving in and out of my beautiful, sexy woman, I pressed my chest to her back, my arms on top of her outstretched arms. "Mm...I'm going to love living with you."

25

ROYALTY

Raini invited me to a girls' trip to an Arizona spa away from our men and children. We had both been busy with the major transitions in our lives and hadn't had any alone time in weeks. Ryder and I moved in with Devin, and we had been living together in mostly harmony the past three months. My parents loved and accepted Devin from that very first day in Okinawa, and our trip overseas had been a success.

Ryder had already begun seventh grade, and as a family we decided that if he really didn't like Oak Ivy Prep, he could transfer to another school for eighth grade or high school. Devin believed that since he would be more involved with the school through his law firm, he could keep an eye on Ryder and believed that his seventh-grade year would be a better experience.

"Ooh, Rain. This whole having to account for my actions to another person is tough," I complained to Raini. We'd just finished yoga and meditation class and were stretched out by the infinity pool. "I'm used to making decisions on my own, and Devin is so gung-ho about being the best man for me and father to Ryder, he is driving me crazy with his constant need for us to discuss everything. I don't know if this is the honeymoon phase or this is who he is with us."

Raini sipped on her fruit drink. "Well, at least he pitches in and helps. I have a spoiled grown-ass man who can't seem to do anything around the house without my opinion or help. I'm like, dude, you were in this house years before you married me."

I laughed. "Look at us, sounding like old married women, complaining about our men, except one of us isn't married."

She smiled. "Yet. Devin will come around."

"I'm not worried about us getting married anytime soon. We've been adjusting to living together, and in time we will make it official. I think of him as my husband anyway. Thankfully, the biggest challenge is learning to rely on each other. Easier for him than me because he's been married before. He and Ryder get along so well, he hasn't had to raise his voice or anything. Meanwhile, I'm still yelling. Devin keeps telling me I give Ryder too many chances instead of sticking firm to a decision. I just think Ry is so crazy about Devin, he'll do whatever he says, even if he doesn't like it."

"I think both are true."

"What? I've always been mean Mommy and you're the nice Tee Rain."

"Yes, because I never say 'no.' But you do let Ryder talk you out of a decision quite often, and fathers aren't going to let that happen, especially with their sons. Tracie loves her daddy, but knows to ask me first if she wants something."

I eased back in my lounge chair by the pool. "For a while I didn't think Ryder or Devin would forgive me. They were both so angry with me. I still can't get over seeing Tre at Devin's office speaking on my behalf."

"I think he was tired of me being worried about you. Plus, he realized that he'd been holding on to his anger toward Devin for too long. They really were close."

"You think they'll ever be friends again?"

"I think so. At the LaSalle annual Fourth of July barbecue, although they didn't speak much except to greet each other, I didn't feel any tension between them. Besides, they better learn, because I'm not trying to miss out on family trips with you because the men can't get along—especially because Ry looks after Tracie like she's his little sister."

"We will just have to do family dinners at each other's homes." I closed my eyes, enjoying the rays of the sun. "Getting away for the weekend was such a good idea. I needed to feel like Royalty. Not Ryder's mama or Devin's woman. Just me."

"Well, you better enjoy your last day of me time, because your men can't wait to see you."

I smiled. "And I can't wait to see them."

※

RAINI DROVE ME HOME, AND INSTEAD OF HEADING TO HER own family, she turned off the motor in our driveway. "I have to use the bathroom."

"I told you not to drink all that water on the plane. And you know once Ry sees you, he's going to want you to stay longer."

"I miss my Ry. I can stay long enough to play a round of *Assassin's Creed*."

I opened the door to an empty home and walked through the living room, calling the names of the two men in my life. No response. "They knew I was coming home this evening. Where did they go?"

"Maybe they're on the deck. It's a nice night." Raini walked past me through the hall that led to the pool and bar area.

Once she opened the door and walked through, she quickly stepped to the side, and I stopped in my tracks. Our backyard had been transformed into a romantic wonderland. The green lushness of the manicured lawn and the clear late September night served as the perfect backdrop for the twinkling white lights and white roses. I adjusted my eyes to see Ryder and Devin, both so freshly groomed and handsome, dressed in similar button-up crisp white shirts and gray pants, standing on the other side of the pool. We were separated by a clear see-through walkway lit with white candles, that had been built and placed across the water.

Sobbing in anticipation and at the sheer beauty of the marriage proposal that Devin had planned for me, I covered my face, and when I lifted my head again, I realized that we were not alone. On either side of the pool were our families. On one side, Devin's parents and Nicholas smiled at me. My knees buckled when I noticed my parents and my big brother waving from the other side. Tre and Tracie sat next to my family. I looked back at Raini. "You knew about this?"

Raini's eyes shone with unshed tears. "Devin asked me to take you away so that he could do all of this for you. Surprise!"

I turned back around, sniffing and wiping my eyes with my finger, trying to preserve my eye makeup. "This is crazy. So, what do I do? What's happening right now?"

Ryder called, "Mama, Daddy has to ask you something important."

Everyone laughed.

Smiling through my tears, I said, "I want to hug all of you, especially my brother." I stared at Devin in wonder. "You did all this?"

He nodded, still quiet.

My brother half-stood before Mama pulled him back down roughly. "Royal, you can hug and talk to us later, your man is waiting for you. Go ahead."

I inhaled deeply when my daddy approached me and extended his arm for me to hold.

"Hey, Daddy."

"Hey, Pumpkin."

"How long did you know?"

"Since your visit with us. We arrived yesterday morning and been here with Ryder and Devin. You're in good hands, Royalty. He's going to do right by you."

"Aww, Daddy, you think so?"

"I know so." He kissed my forehead, much like he always did whenever he wasn't deployed and read me a story at night.

We walked together across the blue pool to a smiling Ryder and serene Devin. "You both look so handsome."

"And you look pretty as always, Mama."

I wore a pale blue strapless sundress, grateful that I opted for the dress instead of the shorts and T-shirt I'd contemplated wearing.

Daddy grasped Devin's hand and shook firmly. "Take care of her."

Devin finally spoke, his voice deep, "Yes, sir. You never have to worry about Ryder and Royalty again."

My dad smiled, hugged me, and walked back across the pool.

Devin lifted both my hands and caressed my knuckles with his full lips.

I said, "I can't believe you pulled all this together in three days."

"I had a little help."

Only wearing flat sandals, I had to stand on my tiptoes to give him a kiss. "Do you know how amazing you are?"

"Mama, you have to wait to kiss him."

I then kissed Ryder on his cheek. "It's okay, I have a kiss for my young handsome man, too."

"Mama." He blushed but didn't wipe off my kiss this time.

Devin squeezed my hands. "Ready for me to ask you?"

I squealed in excitement. "You already know my answer."

"I do know your answer today, I just hope that I am always your answer."

I lifted our clasped hands and pressed them against my heart. "As long as you are on this Earth, it will always be you and only you I want by my side."

His eyes watered.

"I may not always be an easy man to live with, and you will probably curse me at least once a week, but I promise that I will never cheat, forsake you, or lie to you. I need you, I need my son, and I need this life that we are creating together."

I couldn't help but tease him. "You mean our son?"

His grin displayed his beautiful white teeth. "You had ten years to claim him as only your son, give me a little more time to proudly say that Ryder is my son. Can I have that please?"

"I'm cool with that," Ryder chimed in. "I am a Toussaint man."

"Young man," Devin corrected. "You have your whole life to be a man. Enjoy being a boy. You don't have to worry about your mama alone anymore. I'm here now."

"Amen," I heard my mother say aloud.

Devin then reached in his pocket and my heart fluttered in anticipation of the huge rock I always imagined that he would give me. Except instead of a box, he pulled out a thin platinum diamond-encrusted wedding band, and Ryder presented me with a matching man's band on a small black velvet pillow. "I'm asking you not only to be my wife, I'm asking you to be my wife today."

I gasped. "This is my wedding?"

Devin looked nervous while placing my ring next to his on the cushion Ryder held. He picked up my hands again. "Queen, I have been wanting to be your husband since I saw you again at the French Market and the fire still blazed between us. Remember you tried to lie and say you were married to keep me away?"

I could hear Raini's giggle, because she had been there.

"I never told you that I instinctively knew you weren't, because at that moment, I knew you were meant to be my wife. It's why I couldn't help but touch you that day to be sure you were real. And then to discover we already had a son together both brightened my life and broke my heart. Broke my heart that because of my lies, you delivered him on your own, you didn't get to share with me all the little milestones as he grew from a baby to a boy, that you had to be his mother and father."

He stopped talking to look at Ryder, and slow tears caressed both of their cheeks. I tugged on his hands, not wanting him to get caught up in the past and regretful emotions. Devin blinked and refocused on the present, on me.

"You gave me a son. A boy who I'd already wished could be mine—who I'd loved—before I knew he was my flesh and blood. No matter how much I wished our paths had crossed again sooner, God has shown me that we met the moment it was supposed to happen. We met again to explore this insane love that we've been blessed to find. We met again when we did because Ryder needs me now—perhaps more than he did when he was younger. We met again to create and share this beautiful life together, and I don't want to wait a moment longer to call you my wife.

"But if you say you want to wait and have a church wedding or a bigger ceremony..." Devin reached into his pocket again, and this time held a large princess cut platinum ring, even better than the one I'd always envisioned. "I'll place this on your finger for now."

My heart full for this complicated man who simply loved me and our son deeply, I smoothed the lines on his forehead. "Baby, I don't want to wait any longer either to wear your name proudly. I had to suppress the love I felt for you for so long, that when I saw you again, I panicked. Because I knew in that moment, that I wanted you to be my husband. The unbridled joy in your facial expression, your tone, and the way you touched me that day at the market sparked the blazing fire between us that I'd thought had long died." I touched his gorgeous face reverently. "You and I have been on a journey that started almost twelve years ago when I lost a bet and you walked in that bar. A journey in which we had to grow as individuals before coming back together as one. I want to make the most of this life we have and grow old with you. All the people we care about in the world are here in our backyard. You, them, and God is all I need to marry you today."

He clenched his jaw, shaking his head in wonder. "I love you so much."

"And I you."

Tre's father, Judge LaSalle, suddenly appeared before us holding a bible.

I stared incredulously at my very-soon-to-be-husband. "You were able to get the judge to marry us?"

Devin lips curved into the brightest smile and looked across the pool at Tre who had been joined by Raini. "I called in a favor from an old friend. I needed him here on the most important day of my life like we'd always promised each other, and I asked if he thought his father could perform our ceremony."

Raini rested her head on Tre's shoulder and he smiled reassuringly.

I turned back to the man who could make me smile just at the sight of him. My love. My king. My Devin.

Judge LaSalle, with a warm and kind voice, announced, "Shall we get started?"

Devin and I grasped hands again as we gazed into each other's eyes with promises of the upmost passion, respect, care, trust, and above all an undying love.

Until death do us part.

Also by Tiye Love

Unforgettable Kiss (Unforgettable #1)
Unforgettable Man (Unforgettable #2)

Forbidden (Forbidden Trilogy #1)
Forbidden Secrets (Forbidden Trilogy #2)
Forbidden Hearts (Forbidden Trilogy #3)

Endgame (Endgame Trilogy #1)
Game Time (Endgame Trilogy #2)
Game Changer (Endgame Trilogy #3)

VISIT US

Website:
www.gardenavenuepress.com

Twitter:
@GardenAvePress

Facebook
www.facebook.com/GardenAvenuePress

ABOUT THE AUTHOR

TIYE LOVE recalled reading romance ever since she was a young child and would sneak and read the Western love stories her grandmother kept on her bedside table. Although she didn't understand half of the words she read at the time, something about those books captured her attention. As she grew older, her love of romance expanded to other genres, and she became a fan of anything remotely related to reading and books, such as libraries, bookstores, and the coffeeshop around the corner.

She loves to travel and has lived in several cities, including New Orleans, Washington D.C., and Houston, and finds inspiration for her stories from every place she has had the fortune to visit or inhabit. When Tiye is not obsessed with her latest characters, she spends time with herself, family, and friends doing whatever she can to create her best life possible.

www.tiyelovebooks.com

facebook.com/lovetiye
instagram.com/tiye28always

Made in the USA
Middletown, DE
11 January 2021